SPELLBOUND

Prophecy of a Fae
Book Two

BONNIE THOMLEY

FICTION WRITER
Bonnie Thomley

To all of my family, friends, and teachers that have encouraged me along my journey. Thank you for believing in me and inspiring a life of dreaming.

A divide is forged. A line in the sands eternally drawn. What is done cannot be undone.
A battle between good and evil shall decide the fates of all mystica.

PROLOGUE

"Have you seen her?" Fiona asked with a panicked tone in her voice.

"No. I've looked everywhere. She isn't answering her phone either."

"It's not like her to disappear like this. She was acting weird last night when she went to bed."

"What do you mean she was acting weird? What was she doing?"

"Didn't she call you? She calls you every night if you're not staying here."

"No, I never heard from her. I assumed she fell asleep. She was really tired yesterday." Gideon ran his fingers through his hair, frustrated.

"She just seemed a bit on edge. You know, pacing a lot, acting worried. Asked her what was wrong, but she just waved her hand as if to say nothing. After I told her goodnight, she went into her room. That's the last that I saw her."

"Shit. Go ask your mom if she has seen her. I'll go talk to Vincent. Call me if you figure anything out."

Damnit, Brynn. Where was she? She hadn't been acting herself the last few days. She was distant and distracted.

Ouch! Not again... The sharp pain in his chest took him straight to his knees. His tattoo had been doing that for days now. It had to be about Brynn. It was her tattoo. He pulled out his phone and dialed Vincent.

"Hey Gideon. What's up?"

"Hey. Have you heard from Brynn today?"

"No, I haven't. Is everything ok?"

"I don't know. No one has seen her. It's unlike her. She always at least tells someone where she is going."

"Hmm. Find Madeleine. If nothing else Bruce might be able to figure something out. He's got powers far beyond what any of us have."

"Ok, thanks. I'll let you know when I find her."

Gideon hung up the phone and started looking for Madeleine. Hopefully, Fiona had already been able to track her down. His tattoo throbbed once again. Not now. He had to keep going.

He started walking toward the living room. It could be difficult to find someone at the compound. There were always so many people in and out. He was spending a lot of time here lately, but he still wasn't used to it. He could hear the faint sound of voices up ahead, so he picked up the pace.

"Gideon! I was just about to call you. No one has seen her today." Fiona frowned.

Shyan and Madeleine were standing with her looking worried.

"Vincent hasn't heard from her either." He shrugged his shoulders, feeling defeated.

"Gideon. The fairy you and Brynn went to visit in the woods. Do you remember her name? Brynn wasn't sure and said that I should ask you." Madeleine had been meaning to ask him this already, but it kept slipping her mind.

"Yeah. That makes sense. Brynn is terrible with names. The fairy we went to see called herself Gwen."

"Shit! Someone go find Bruce." Everyone froze in place. Her sudden panic startled everyone. After a second, Gideon began to run for Bruce's room.

"Hurry!" Madeleine's voice disappeared behind him.

ONE

"How do you know about Gwen anyway?" Madeleine asked harshly. She did nothing to sugarcoat her tone. None of this was making any sense.

"Some old fairy told Brynn about her. She said that Gwen could have information about where the former court members might have gone. Of course, Brynn was on board. Who is she?"

"Stellah." She sighed. "Gwen is no fairy. She is a witch. An old, powerful witch at that. We need to find Brynn quickly."

As if on cue, Bruce burst into the room. His wild hair sticking out all around him.

"Let's take your truck, Gideon. You remember how to get there?" Even though he hadn't been part of the conversation, he knew exactly what was going on.

Gideon nodded and followed Bruce to the front door.

"Call if you all need more people. In the meantime, I'm gonna find that bitch Stellah." Madeleine called out.

"Go get 'er, baby!" Bruce shouted as he and Gideon walked out of the door.

"Thank you for waiting for me to get here." Bruce said as they pulled onto the main road. "Gwen is incredibly powerful. She's a bit of a master of disguise as well I am afraid. It will probably take both of us to track her down."

"How could I not tell she was a witch? I'm an animal for shit's sake. I should have sniffed her out before we were even out of the truck. Fairy face or not." Gideon's husky southern twang would have made Bruce chuckle on any other occasion.

"She is incredibly old and very seasoned. Old magic can often be the most dangerous magic. I imagine she is quite proficient in masking her scent. A witch doesn't make it to her age without being a master of illusion. They always have a target on their backs."

Gideon pulled off of the main road onto a narrow dirt trail in the woods. If he had blinked for too long, he might have missed it. Hundreds of people drove past this spot every day. None of them probably even noticed this trail. Hell, he only found it this time because he was tracking Brynn.

The ride was bumpy and he couldn't help but think of taking this ride with Brynn. She thanked him for coming with her on that trip, but he wouldn't have been anywhere else. Quyen teased him about how happy he was to spend the day with her. The energy of her aura alone was enough for him to want to be close. Her personality and that beautiful face... well those just added to the pot. To say he was smitten was an understatement.

He rubbed his chest. His tattoo burned. She was in danger. He needed to find her soon.

They neared the spot where they parked the truck before. He slowed the old Chevy down considerably. Gwen's house wasn't up ahead in the distance like it was last time. This was definitely the right place. He could smell it. This wasn't right, though.

"Why are we stopping?" Bruce finally asked.

Gideon was just sitting there dumbfounded. It didn't make sense.

"We are here. But it isn't the same as last time."

"Not the same? Something is missing?"

"Yeah, dude. The whole fucking house is missing!"

Bruce didn't mistake Gideon's emotions for weakness. It was pure rage. Any creature within a five-mile radius could probably feel it. It was amazing that he hadn't shifted into a bear by now.

"Perhaps there was a trail along the way that we should have turned down. Let's backtrack and see if we can find it." Bruce's voice remained steady and level.

"I promise you that we are in the right place. I realize how it looks, but I am not wrong about this."

"I don't mean to doubt you son, but you are right. This doesn't look ideal. How can you be so certain that we are in the right place? There is nothing here."

"Because Brynn is my mate! That's how I know." Gideon shouted. He banged his fists on the steering wheel before getting out of the car. Dust and leaves flew around him as he slammed the door shut.

Bruce gasped. Having a mate of a different race was unheard of. This kind of thing didn't happen. Mates were determined by God and navigated by the stars. In all his hundreds of years he had not heard of such a thing occurring. He quickly exited the truck and joined Gideon ahead on the trail.

"Don't look at me like that." Gideon sighed. "Trust me, I know. Imagine my internal conflict when I found out. This kinda thing just don't happen. Anyway, no one else knows. But now you must understand why I'm so certain that we are in the right place. I can remember every detail about every moment I have had with her. It's instinct."

Bruce nodded. Warlocks didn't have star mates like many of the other races. They had the freedom to choose. He always thought that having a choice was better. Without a choice, he wouldn't have Madeleine in his life. He could appreciate the type of pull star assigned mates had to each other, though. Fairies didn't have star mates either, which made all of this much stranger.

"Then focus on that energy, young man. Focus on feeling her. Let your soul seek out your mate. Close your eyes. Is she near?"

Gideon closed his eyes and began to focus like Bruce suggested. He thought about Brynn. Her smile, her shimmer, her complete unwillingness to back down. He knew that she was his mate the first day they met. When they were training before the battle, it took everything in him not to make a move. Mate or not, she was rare. She was his and she didn't even know it yet.

There it was. It felt like a heartbeat. He focused, trying to force his heart to beat in the same rhythm. Synchronicity.

"She's close." His voice was raspy. The desperation he felt was something he wasn't used to. No girl had made him feel this crazy before. Especially a fairy. He used to always joke around, often referring to them as "sparkle girls."

Bruce's pupils dilated wide like an excited cat and he began to softly chant. Gideon didn't know what was happening. Before Brynn, he kept his distance from fairies. He had never met a warlock before. His spell casting knowledge was pretty low. The lowest if he had to guess.

The ground suddenly began to tremble and Bruce was voicing a low growl. A piercing noise ripped through the air taking Gideon down to his knees. He covered his ears with his hands.

The air around them blurred. Gideon squinted his eyes, trying to find Bruce. He was still in a trance. Everything was so disorienting. Were they in a tornado? Gideon didn't even try to get up. The sound continued but up ahead things were beginning to sharpen and come into view.

Gwen's house.

"I told you we were in the right place." Gideon shouted once the noise stopped. He couldn't tell how loud he was. His ears were ringing.

He quickly hopped up and ran toward the house. If his knees were shaky, he wouldn't know. His adrenaline had kicked into high gear. A swarm of bees could be unleashed on him right now and he probably wouldn't feel it.

"Use caution! It could be booby trapped." Bruce yelled behind him somewhere.

Gideon laughed. Nothing about him was cautious. That certainly wasn't going to change today.

As he got to the porch, he picked up his foot and planted it firmly left of center on the front door near the knob. It flew open with ease.

"Brynn! Are you in here?" he shouted as he crossed the threshold.

He listened closely as he made his way through the house. Not a peep. He could feel that she was here, so he kept searching. He called out to her a few more times with no answer. Hopefully, she wasn't hidden like the damn house was.

Bruce was scampering around. He was mumbling something about witch ingredients. Gideon assumed he was heading to either the kitchen or the medicine cabinet.

"Where are you, Brynn?" he said in a whisper, almost only for himself to hear. "I can feel you. You have to be close."

As he rounded the corner of the living room to head down the hallway, he saw her. She was sitting on the floor with her arms wrapped around her legs. She was rocking slightly back and forth. Her hair was wild.

Gideon squatted down in front of her. She didn't even blink. She just sat there with a faraway look in her eyes.

"Brynn?" Gideon placed his hand on Brynn's arm. "What happened? Are you okay?"

She just sat there.

"Bruce! Get in here!" Gideon yelled as loudly as he could.

Within seconds, Bruce came running into the room.

"You found her. Oh dear…"

"Why is she like this?"

"She appears to be spellbound, I'm afraid. We need to get her home quickly so I can address this properly."

"Get the truck started. I'll meet you there." He tossed Bruce the keys.

Bruce caught the keys in the air and nodded as he scurried out of the room. Gideon turned his attention back to Brynn. He brushed a piece of hair off of her face. She didn't even flinch.

"I'm gonna pick you up and carry you to the truck. Once we get you home we will get this figured out."

She still didn't respond. He picked her up and carried her like a baby out of the house. She didn't stir. She was so small in his arms. It hurt him to see her so helpless. Brynn was destined to be a queen for a reason. She was tough... tougher than all of this for sure.

When he got outside, the truck was started and Bruce had moved to the passenger seat. He pushed the driver door open. Gideon slid into the truck with Brynn and tucked her in between the two of them. He strapped her seatbelt on and threw the truck into drive.

"I'm more of a feral beast than I am a wood sprite. You're gonna need to explain being spellbound to me Catman."

"Catman?" Bruce chuckled.

"I don't mean anything by it. You know you're like a cat."

"When someone is spellbound, they are in almost a catatonic state. They can't respond.

She won't eat, sleep, or drink as long as she is like this. It cannot be maintained long term."

"How do we fix it?"

"First I've got to identify what type of spell it is. Once I narrow it down, I can gather the items that will be necessary to make the antidote. In the meantime, I need you to keep her safe and her environment calm. She does not need to be distressed."

"I hear ya. I'm not just walking around raging out all of the time. Don't judge me based on this interaction alone. I'm usually a pretty laid-back guy."

"No judgment. I know how important she is to you. I would walk through the gates of hell just to get a glimpse of her aunt without hesitation."

Gideon pulled the truck back onto the highway. He rubbed the side of his face. He was exhausted. At least he had Brynn now. Hopefully, Bruce was as high of a warlock as it seemed.

"When we get back, I suggest taking Brynn to her room and putting her in bed. Make her comfortable. I assume that you will be staying?"

"Of course. I'm not letting her out of my sight ever again."

"Good. She needs that. I will do a few evaluations once you have her in place."

"That's perfect. I need to call Vincent and let him know what's going on. If you don't mind staying with her until I am back."

"Yes, of course. I do not mind waiting with her."

They turned down the driveway and made their way up to the house. Once they were close, you could see people coming outside.

"I will answer their questions. Just get Brynn to her room."

"Won't they stop me?"

"Ha!" Bruce cackled. "You're much bigger than any of them. I'd like to see them try."

Gideon cracked a smile for the first time all day. Bruce was right. He needed to man up. Brynn wouldn't want a weak mate.

TWO

"Sorry that took so long. How is our patient?" Bruce asked in huff as he shut the bedroom door behind him.

"No change. She seems comfortable though. I'm guessing there were a lot of questions down there, but were there any helpful answers?"

"Madeleine tracked down the fairy who told Brynn about Gwen. Unfortunately, she was dead so we have no leads on Gwen."

"Well hell, this day just keeps getting better don't it?"

"By the way, Vincent was already on the phone with Shyan, so he knows the scoop. He should be here soon if you want to get a breather or take a break."

"Nah, I'm good right here. I just don't want to let her out of my site. We could have lost her today."

"Don't you worry, it takes quite a bit to offend me. I'm not going to do anything too rigorous this evening. While time is of the essence, we cannot afford to keep her in a stressed state. The trouble is her emotionless condition makes it difficult to gauge how she is feeling."

"Where do we start?" Gideon rubbed his face. The stubble on his jaw line scratched his hand.

"I have a few basic tinctures with me. I'm not expecting anything spectacular, but it is a good jumping off point."

"Could any of it make her worse?"

"No. Everything I am trying is safe."

"Alright then." Gideon sat down at the

foot of the bed and gave Bruce some space to work.

Gideon watched Bruce work. His fluffy hair bounded around as he applied tinctures on Brynn's pressure points and lips. The room was beginning to smell like an old apothecary. He rubbed his hands together and held them over Brynn's body. His brow furrowed.

"Like I expected, unfortunately. This spell is more advanced that the tinctures that I had on hand can counter. I will have to try something more extensive tomorrow."

"Let me know if I can do anything to help. No matter how small or large the task."

"Just keep her comfortable. I already know that you will."

"I will. See ya tomorrow."

Bruce showed himself out and Gideon sat down next to Brynn.

"I don't know if you can hear me or not. You're gonna be okay. I won't stop until you are. And whoever did this to you will pay."

He grabbed her hairbrush from the bedside tablet and began bushing her hair. When he was finished, he tied it in a loose braid. He rubbed her arms, hands, and feet with lotion. He grabbed her favorite blue blanket and draped it over her.

A knock at the door caught his attention and he kissed her on the forehead before getting up. Shyan smiled when he opened the door.

"I know you don't want to leave her. I brought you some food." She handed him a tray with a piece of foil covering it and utensils on top.

"Thank you. I'm starving."

He hadn't even thought about food since finding Brynn. Now that the aroma of homemade food filled his nostrils, he was acutely aware of his hunger level. His stomach let out an almost perfectly timed growl. Shyan smiled.

Gideon stepped away from the door and motioned for Shyan to follow him in. She walked over to Brynn and put her hand on her cheek.

"My sweet baby." she said softly. "Who has done this to you?"

Tears formed in the corners of her emerald green eyes. She knew Brynn's destiny came with its fair share of danger. To see it on this level made it so much more real. She started into her daughter's blank eyes and felt fury.

She got up abruptly and walked back toward the door.

"If you need anything, just text one of us. We won't hover, but we are here to help."

"I appreciate that. Don't feel like you can't come check on her just because I'm in here with her." Gideon replied, already removing the foil from his tray.

Shyan nodded as she turned and walked away. Gideon was relieved to have the meal. He meant it when he told her that he was starving. He just hadn't been willing to leave Brynn's side to do anything about it.

The plate looked amazing. There were two pieces of fried chicken, mashed potatoes with brown gravy, green beans with bacon, a biscuit, and five chocolate chip cookies. One thing for sure was these fairies always ate well and made sure everyone was fed. Some sort of southern fairy hospitality.

Gideon's phone chirped and he pulled it out of his pocket before sitting down on the bed. It was Quyen. He should have called her to check in already. She was probably worried.

"Just checking in. ♥" Quyen wrote.

"Sorry, I should have already. We found her and are back at her house. I need to stay with her for right now. She is spellbound. Do you know what that means?"

"Yes, I do. How bad is she?"

"I'm glad you do cause I sure didn't know. Thank God Bruce was with me. He is trying to figure out what spell it is so he can fix it. What he tried tonight didn't work. He'll be back tomorrow."

"I know this is extra hard for you right now, Gid. I'm sorry."

"What do you mean? Because I am the

one that took her to Gwen's house?"

"No. The mate thing. I know the prophecy, remember?"

"Why didn't you tell me? A heads up would have been nice. This has had me going out of my mind, Q."

"You know I can't. I'm not allowed to interfere."

"I know. I still have to give you a hard time, though."

"Keep your head up. It's gonna get better."

He tossed his phone down on the bed. He hoped that she was speaking from a place of knowledge and not just trying to make him feel better. The last thing he needed was for someone just to placate him.

What he really needed was sleep. After making sure Brynn was in a comfortable position, he turned off the lights and snuggled up close to her. He was out in no time.

The next few days went by rather

quickly.

Bruce was in and out a lot trying different things and taking notes. He kept sending fairies off on different missions to gather exotic ingredients. It was busy. All the while, Gideon made sure Brynn was clean, comfortable, and as pampered as she could be in her current state. He changed her clothes, kept up with her skincare routine, and even painted her nails.

However, each day that passed posed a bigger problem. With Brynn out of commission, no one was in charge.

"Brynn appointed you to be her partner. You should take over for her." Shyan told Gideon while checking on Brynn.

"While I can appreciate where you are coming from Shyan, you and I both know that these fairies are not gonna take too kindly to me bossing them around. It should be you. You know them. They trust you."

"I don't know about that Gideon. Do you think Brynn would be okay with that? She and I haven't always seen eye to eye. I don't want her to feel like I was trying to replace her."

"I think she'd be fine with it. You are the only one on our side that they will listen to. Vincent is a vampire. Madeleine was cast out. Fiona is too immature. I promise you everyone would agree with me."

Shyan nodded and left the room.

"You're right. Everyone would agree with you." Bruce agreed quietly while continuing to try to heal Brynn.

"Thanks. Any luck?"

"Not really. This magic is complicated. We need to either find this witch or find out who put her up to hurting Brynn."

"Does Madeleine have any leads?"

"I'm afraid not. No one has seen Gwen. It's pretty hard to narrow down a suspect when every single former court member wants her dead."

"Maybe we missed something in the woods."

"Are you thinking of going back?" Bruce

looked up from his work, surprised.

"No. I am thinking about sending someone else, though. My brother is an excellent tracker. Maybe it's time I brought him in on this. Could you stay with Brynn until I get back? Raef doesn't keep a phone. This is a favor I will have to ask for in person."

"I will stay with her. Do what you need to."

Gideon kissed Brynn on the cheek before grabbing his phone.

"I'll be back soon, sweetheart."

"Good luck!" Bruce shouted as he left.

Normally Gideon would enjoy a quiet drive. Today, he was hoping to make it a quick trip. He wanted to be there when Brynn opened her eyes.

He made a sharp turn onto a dirt road about five miles down the main road. The road was badly eroded. He could never make this trek in something other than his truck. Raef liked it this way. It made trespassers a lot less likely.

The road took a winding path into the woods. The pass was narrow before eventually opening up to a meadow of sorts that still had plenty of tree cover. It was the perfect place to be tucked away.

"Hey little bro!" Raef shouted as Gideon hopped out of the truck. His surfer accent was always such a stark contrast to Gideon's southern drawl. "What brings you out my way?"

He opened his arms to hug Gideon.

"I don't suppose you have talked to Quyen at all this week?"

"No, man. I think you might be the first person I have talked to all week. She okay?"

"Quyen is fine. Long story very short, Brynn went missing. I found her in the woods at a house that ended up belonging to a witch. Now Brynn is spellbound which pretty much means that she is fucking catatonic. The warlock is trying to break the spell, but it's not working."

"Dang little bro. That's a lot to take in. What can I do to help?"

"I need to either find this witch or find who employed her. We need to know what kind of spell it is."

"You already know I'm in. Where do you want me to start?"

"The woods. I can take you to the spot. That's the only lead I have."

"I'm ready when you are dude. Let's find this bitch."

"Thanks man."

"Come on, Gid. Anything for my little bro. Plus, you know how much I love the thrill of the hunt. Let me run in the house and grab a few things. I'll be right out."

Gideon hopped into his truck and waited for Raef. If anyone could find something, it was Raef. Hopefully there would be something to find. He didn't wait all these years to find his mate only to watch her slowly die.

"Thanks, man." Gideon said to Raef when he opened the passenger door and hopped into the truck.

Raef nodded as he tossed his duffel bag into the backseat. He was prepared to camp in the woods until he found a clue if need be. He'd never turn down a chance to work in nature. Besides, if he wanted to take a nice lion jog at sunset, he could out amongst the tree cover. No one would see him.

He loved shifting. Connecting with his animal side, as he called it. Gideon was a lot more conservative about it. He would shift to train and fight, but rarely for fun. Even Quyen liked to shift and have some cat time. Raef used to give him a tough time about it when they were kids, but not so much anymore.

"It smells gnarly out here bro." Raef animatedly remarked when Gideon parked outside Gwen's house. "I haven't even made it out of the truck yet and I can smell it."

"What's it smell like to you?"

"Witch shit." He laughed as he opened the truck door and hopped out. Gideon followed suit.

"Before you shift, which I know you're aching to do, let's walk the grounds and talk."

Raef chuckled and nodded. Gideon was right. He was aching to shift and begin his investigation. He could contain himself for a few more minutes, though. As long as his brother wasn't too long winded.

They made their way to the house. It was still empty. Gwen wasn't stupid enough to come back here. Not yet at least.

"We need to find out who else has been here. Especially within a few days of Brynn being here."

"I got it dude. You know I won't stop until the job is done."

"Thanks, man. Let me know if you need anything and especially when you find something."

"I'll call you soon."

"You don't have a phone."

"I brought a throw away just for you little bro!"

Before Gideon could respond, Raef shifted. Gideon laughed. He knew his brother couldn't resist much longer.

"See you soon you crazy son of a bitch."

Raef purred and hit Gideon with his tail before running out of view.

THREE

"How's my girl doing?" Gideon asked Bruce as he walked back into Brynn's room.

"No change so far." Bruce remarked. "How did things go with your brother?"

"Good. Raef has a nose like no other. He won't stop until he figures something out."

"I'm glad to hear that because I'm afraid we do need major help. Nothing I have tried has made a bit of difference. I think we are dealing with magic that is rare."

Gideon sighed as he sat down on the edge of the bed. He looked at Brynn for a moment before pushing a piece of hair off of her forehead. She sat there with those river blue eyes staring past him, still in an almost frozen state.

"Well hell Catman. That's definitely not what I wanted to hear. It's okay though. We can count on my brother."

He kissed Brynn on the top of the head.

"I promise." He whispered into her ear.

A stern knock at the door startled him.

"Come on in." Gideon announced.

Shyan scurried into the room looking panicked. Her blonde hair, which was normally neat and groomed, looked wild.

"What's wrong, Shyan?" Bruce asked.

"I just got word of an attack. Details are sketchy, but it sounds like the suspect is a former court member."

"I was afraid this would start with Brynn being out of commission. What's next?"

Gideon asked while braiding Brynn's hair.

It took Shyan a minute to respond as she studied Gideon. She didn't know how she felt about Brynn being with a shifter. It would make her life harder. It had already been tough enough for her. He was big, muscular, and covered in tattoos. Now though, she could see the softness in him. The love.

He had made sure Brynn was taken care of through this spellbound state. He had been bathing her, clothing her, even doing her hair this entire time. Shyan noticed that he had even painted her nails. Without anyone even asking him to do so. There was a devotion there that she hadn't noticed until now.

"Vincent is on his way to investigate. He's supposed to check in soon."

"Is the victim?" Bruce seemed to not want to finish his question.

"Dead."

"Any witnesses?"

"It sounds like there is a potential

witness. Again, the details are a bit hazy so I really don't know right now."

"I imagine they are going to start taking more chances once word of Brynn's condition gets around." Bruce suggested.

"Probably so. I'd see it as a perfect opportunity if I were them."

"I'll give you an update when I have one. Thanks for taking such good care of her, Gideon."

"No need to thank me. I'm just happy to be here with her."

"I believe that." Shyan smiled and left the room.

"I'm going out for a few supplies. Let me know if you need anything." Bruce said as he closed the bag he kept all of his warlock goodies in.

"Will do."

Gideon kissed Brynn's head and moved around to sit beside her in the bed.

"I don't know if you can hear me or not.

I know that you're gonna make it through this. You're the toughest girl I know... and I know some bad asses."

He pulled out his phone and called Quyen. He knew she could take care of herself but he still liked to check in with her.

He tried hard not to pester her about the prophecy. He knew that she couldn't tell him anything. It wasn't fair for him to pressure her. That fact didn't keep him from wanting to.

Their conversation had been pretty basic. They discussed Brynn's condition, Raef's mission, and the recent fairy attack.

"Hey Gid?" Quyen asked as they were getting off of the phone.

"Yeah?"

She hesitated a moment before taking a breath... almost like she was holding something back.

"It's almost over. Be patient."

He was quiet for a moment as he

thought about her words.

"Love you, cuz. I'll call ya soon."

"Love you too." She said before hanging up the phone.

He wanted to ask her so many things. He didn't though. What she gave him was a little hope and he needed that right now.

"We're almost out of the woods, darlin." He stood up and stretched his legs.

He pulled out his phone to send Vincent a text. He was happy to be watching over his mate, but it did make him feel a bit isolated.

"I heard about the attack. Let me know if I can help."

•　　　•　　　•

Vincent looked down at his phone and saw a message from Gideon. He wished that he could take him up on his offer to help.

These fairies were just too untrusting. It was hard enough for him to get them to talk to him because he was part vampire. If he wasn't a fairy also, he would have gotten nowhere.

"Thanks, bud. How's my girl today?"

"Beautiful as always. Hoping for some good news soon."

Vincent was hoping for some good news too. He hadn't told anyone yet, but this wasn't just one attack. He was standing in front of three dead fairies. Innocent lives taken because they wouldn't side with the crooked court members.

He feared these attacks would only increase until Brynn was back in power. They might not admit it, but they feared Brynn. Her angelic lineage meant favor from God in a lot of their eyes. Plus, word had started getting around that she and Gideon were favored by the stars. It was such an ancient concept that many fairies thought was just folklore nonsense, but the older ones knew it wasn't.

That was another reason he knew she was going to pull through this. Surely the stars would not have branded her and spoken to her the way they did if she were not special. Why would they let a special mystica slowly rot away and die? What purpose would that serve? The stars were supposed to be there to guide and watch over the mystica. That was the deal with God.

The stars wouldn't waste their time like that. They were billions of years old. Truth be told, if all mystica knew the truth about the stars, things would be very different. Those that knew weren't allowed to speak on it. It would disrupt the natural order of things.

He knew the origin, though. It was in his blood. Stars were angels. Concentrated energy, celestial beings keeping watch over the world. His angel blood allowed him to see the truth of it all. Soon, that moment would happen for Brynn. Knowing her, the stars had something special in store for her once it came time for their big reveal.

Vincent knelt down next to one of the three fairies in front of him. He didn't know any of them, but he mourned the loss just the same. He placed his palm on her forehead and recited a spell. Once he was finished, her body slowly began fading. Leaving this plane and entering the afterlife.

He continued this magic on the next two fairies. Once they were gone, he walked back to his car. He got in and sighed. This was only the beginning. He knew more death awaited them. There would be another fight. He could feel it. He just didn't know when or who the opponent would be.

The weight was large. Like he told Brynn, special wings come with a special responsibility. He had been given a second chance to be with his family and he was damned if he was going to let it be ripped apart again.

He cranked the car and headed back toward the fairy compound. Normally he would call Shyan and let her know he was on his way back, but he wasn't ready to answer questions. This attack was worse than they expected it to be and he didn't have a lot of answers. He needed time to gather his thoughts before he made it back.

When he pulled back up to the compound, Shyan greeted him outside.

"I'm not trying to bombard you,

sweetheart. I just wanted to talk before everyone inside is around."

"You aren't bombarding me. Sorry I didn't call on my way home. I was just trying to gather my thoughts. Three fairies are dead. I didn't know any of them. It was messy. Unnecessary."

"Savages. I was worried this would happen. Once they hear about Brynn... this is bad, Vincent."

"I know. We have to act fast or things will get out of hand quickly. Any updates on Brynn's condition?"

"Nothing good. Whatever spell she is under is powerful. Bruce has thrown the kitchen sink at it but nothing. Gideon's brother is at Gwen's location in the woods looking for clues. He claims his brother has a powerful nose. He seems very confident."

"I hope he's right. How are you handling the duties?"

Shyan sighed and shrugged her shoulders. Vincent noticed that her normally heavy black eyeliner had been swapped for a lighter style. Her lids were a bit puffy. She was trying to hide the fact that she had been crying.

"I hate it. The stress and anxiety that come along with it... I don't know how she does it."

Vincent smiled and put his arm around Shyan's shoulders. She leaned her head into the crook of his neck. She inhaled deeply. He smelled like a campfire and sandalwood.

"You're a strong woman, Shyan. I know you can handle it. Besides, it will be temporary. You raised a strong, stubborn girl. She wouldn't accept going out like this."

She sniffled.

"You know I'm right."

She nodded.

"Let's get into the house. I'm sure everyone has questions and we need to come up with a game plan." She grabbed his hand and began walking toward the front door.

He was happy to walk beside her. In

the midst of so much chaos, sometimes he felt awestruck that he was here, back with his wife and family. It was a dream that he never thought would come true. It made him more determined than ever to make sure Brynn pulled through. He just got her back.

FOUR

Three days had passed since the attack happened. Things were tense. An unspoken worry hung in the air. One that kept everyone on edge. Everyone was worried about when and where the next attack would be, but no one had anything to go on.

"Fiona, could you run by my house and grab a few supplies?" Vincent asked as he appeared at Fiona's doorway.

She was sitting on her bed writing in her journal. She had become pretty withdrawn since Brynn became spellbound. She twirled her platinum blonde hair around her finger, twisting and twisting. It was a habit she'd had since she was a little girl.

"Sure. Just give me a list."

"Ok. I'll text it to you. Thanks sweetie." He called out as he was already walking away.

"Love you too." She mumbled to herself as she rolled her eyes.

All anyone seemed to care about lately was Brynn. The day Brynn disappeared was the day Fiona started going unnoticed. She shoved her ear buds in her ears and grabbed her bag. Ear buds and current phones used to be off limits, but that had changed since the court dissolved. It was nice not feeling so antiquated.

She walked downstairs, hopped into one of the cars in the driveway, and headed to Vincent's house. She chose to take the silver Mustang. None of the girls drove it very often. They always said it had too much power, but that's what she liked best. She slowly pulled down the driveway. Once she hit the main road, she hit the gas and she was gone.

The closer she got to Vincent's house, the more annoyed she became. Was this all she was good for? Running errands? Doing the chores no one else wanted to do? She gassed it some more and sped down the highway, leaving some of her angst behind her.

The tires screeched as she pulled into Vincent's driveway. Max opened the front door before she made it all the way out of the car.

"I forgot that you might be here." Fiona quipped as she shut the car door.

"You alone?" Max inquired.

"Yeah. I gotta get somethings for my dad."

Max nodded and moved out of her way.

"You look like shit." She told Max as she walked past him and into the kitchen.

"Great to see you too, sparkle bunny."

"That's what friends are for. And sparkle bunny?" She ignored his sarcasm as she started grabbing things for Vincent.

Max walked over and grabbed her phone. He glanced at the list and gave it back to her before grabbing things.

"Friends huh? I sure haven't heard from you. My friends usually call or text me."

She looked at him and shrugged. "I don't know. I guess it's a bit weird. Well, not like weird, but more... awkward."

"I broke up with your sister, not you."

She stopped grabbing things for a moment and pondered.

"I don't even know why it's awkward. No one should care. Vincent still hangs out with you. Hell, no one even knows that I exist now that Brynn is out of her mind. I might as well be a ghost. At least then I wouldn't have to be running errands and checking off things on everyone else's to-do lists."

"I doubt that it's that severe, Fi."

"What? People ignoring me or Brynn being a shut in?"

"You. I don't care about her." He

snapped. "Sorry."

"I'm not exaggerating. In the last three days, I have only been spoken to once. That was today when my dad asked me to run this errand. I am invisible, dude."

"You're definitely not invisible, Fiona. Look at you. You are a rainbow. You're beautiful. Don't let them bring you down."

She smiled shyly. Max moved a little closer to her. Her heart fluttered as she contemplated her next move. She got nervous and moved away.

"I need to get these things back before he starts calling." She stuttered a bit as she grabbed the last thing on her list.

Her arm brushed up against his as she grabbed a solar powered emergency radio out of the drawer he was standing next to. Goosebumps ran down her arms. He was cold to the touch.

"I'll help you bring everything to the car." Max said as he turned to lead her out.

She nodded and followed along behind

him. He opened the front door for her. Instead of walking out, he stood close to the doorway with his arm stretched across, almost too close for Fiona to pass by.

She blushed as she squeezed past him. Who knew where his shirt was. It was hard for her to not look at his abs. Max was in good shape. She could have sworn he flexed as she brushed up against his chest on her way out.

He rushed past her once she was outside. He had her door opened before she even made it off the front porch.

"Vampire speed." He winked at her.

She dropped her items in the backseat and shut the door.

"You should come by again soon. I've missed you. It would be nice to see you again. I could cook you some dinner. Maybe we could watch a movie or something. Hang out like old times."

She sat down in the driver seat and he shut her door.

"You should drive this car more. You

look good in it."

"You should start wearing a shirt." She smiled. "See ya later."

She backed out of the driveway and sped back to the compound. She was a silver blur in no time. What was that? She forgot that Max was still living there. Even so, she wasn't prepared for that type of behavior from him. He was flirting with her.

God help her, she was flirting too. Was that something she wanted to pursue or was she just mad at her sister? Whatever it was, she wasn't going to be able to stop thinking about it. She had never been interested in him before. Of course, she was with Drake back then. And she never noticed how nice his body was.

She shook her head. She couldn't keep thinking about it. She was still in a trance when she pulled back up to her house. After she walked in and put the items on the kitchen table, she went to look for Vincent. She popped her head into his study and bedroom, but he wasn't there.

She figured he must be in Brynn's

room. She rolled her eyes. Definitely not going in there. She went to her room instead and sat down on the bed. She pulled out her phone and sent Vincent a text letting him know where he could find everything.

"Thanks. Sorry I wasn't there to help you. There has been another attack. I'm there now."

"Need any help?"

"No thanks, sweetie. See you tonight."

Fiona didn't reply. Vincent got a sinking feeling in his stomach when he realized she wasn't going to say anything else. He offended her. That hadn't been his intention. He already had one daughter in bad shape, he couldn't risk another.

Two fairies lay at his feet. It looked like they were attacked in the middle of eating lunch. There was food still on the table. Some sort of salad with grilled chicken and figs. Both of their throats were slit. Their wrists and ankles were bound with vines.

Vincent walked around the neighborhood looking for witnesses. There wasn't a soul in sight. He made his way back to the crime scene. He looked again for clues and came up with nothing. He needed help. He pulled out his phone and dialed the only person he thought might actually be able to help him right now. He just hated having to ask..

"Hey Vincent. What's up?" Gideon answered on the first ring.

"I could use your help. There's been another attack. There are no witnesses and I have nothing. Do you think you could come down here and sniff it out?"

Gideon chuckled for a moment. A vampire asking a shifter to sniff something out. This had to be a first.

"Text me the address. I'll head there now."

Gideon hated leaving Brynn, but he needed to see a little action. Besides, Bruce wanted to try a few things today, so he would be there with her for several hours.

When the address came through, he kissed her on the cheek and grabbed his jacket.

"Be back soon." He whispered in her ear.

"She's in good hands." Bruce called as Gideon opened the door.

"That's why I'm heading out. See you soon." Gideon made a beeline for the door.

Once he got in his truck, he punched the address into his GPS. According to the map, it looked like a pretty isolated area. No wonder there were no witnesses.

He thought about Raef on his drive. Wondering how he was doing. Had he found anything? He was hoping to have heard from him already. It would happen at the right time. After Quyen's ominous parting words the other day, he was feeling a little more optimistic.

Vincent was waiting outside when Gideon pulled up. It was an old country house that looked like it might have been hand built. The area was pretty desolate. He had to take five different dirt roads to get out to the location.

"Thanks for coming." Vincent said, squinting his eyes in the sun. Shyan kept the sunlight spell cast on him these days. Even with that, it was still a bit uncomfortable. Like a slight tingle just under the skin.

"Happy to help." Gideon extended his hand and shook Vincent's. "Whataya got?"

"Shit." Vincent sighed. "No witnesses. No leads of any kind. Not even a damn clue. Unless they slit their own throats with invisible knives after binding their ankles and wrists, I have no explanation."

They walked into the house and Gideon quickly darted his eyes around.

"I figured you must be pretty desperate. A vampire asking a shifter to sniff something out? You know how good your sense of smell is. You might even have me beat."

"Yeah, you might be right. Our sense of smell is quite different from each other, though. Maybe you can pick up something I can't."

"I'll give it a shot." Gideon closed his eyes and focused on the room. The bodies.

Was there something there that didn't belong? Bread, deli meat, fairy blood. Fairy blood had such a distinct smell. It smelled sweet... almost like maple syrup in a copper dispenser. It was easy to see why vampires were such a worry for them.

He wondered if it was difficult for Vincent to be around.

"What do you smell?" Vincent asked him.

"Fairy blood, lunch, jasmine, charcoal, and something... spicy."

Gideon opened his eyes. He didn't know what the last few meant. Hopefully, Vincent would.

"I was afraid of that."

"Why? What is it?"

"A wood fairy. Easier to figure out a suspect, but the magic is far more advanced."

"I don't think it's related to Brynn. None of these smells were at Gwen's house. There would have been a shred of something."

"Damn. I'll tell ya Gideon, I've been praying for a breakthrough. I know it sounds crazy." Vincent waved his hands. "I know vampires are damned. But I still have angelic blood. It's a confusing way to live life."

"I'd imagine so. Don't get down about it. I think our luck is about to turn around. Raef will come through. He really is the best at what he does."

"Thanks for coming all the way out here. And thanks for taking care of my little girl."

"Both are my pleasure. She's a pretty special girl. I'm not talking about the prophecy either."

Gideon walked back to his truck and headed home to Brynn. He was glad that Vincent called him. The fresh air was nice. He turned the radio volume up as he pulled out of the driveway. The country station came in good out in this rural area. Very fitting. He glanced in his rear-view mirror and saw Vincent pull out his cell phone before walking back in the house.

Vincent closed the door behind him

and sent a text to Max.

"Looks like we have a wood fairy on our hands."

He promised to keep him updated. He kept it short and sweet. Hopefully, Max wouldn't ask too many questions. Anything surrounding Brynn was off topic for them. They never talked about it... there was just a mutual understanding. He would definitely be upset to hear about Gideon.

Max was still a young vampire. Vincent didn't want to do anything to risk their relationship. Max still had so much left to learn. For now, he would walk on eggshells for a bit. It wasn't ideal, but Max was his responsibility. He sighed before kneeling down beside the latest causalities. One by one he released them into the ether.

After they were gone, he headed home to Shyan. He had to find a way to predict when and where the attacks were going to come.

FIVE

"Hello?" Max answered his phone with a rough voice. He had been asleep.

"Hey. It's Fiona. Um..." She hesitated. "Is it too late for me to come over?"

"I'll never say no to a late-night visit from a hot blonde." Max chuckled. "I'll unlock the front door. Just come on in when you get here."

She hung up the phone spend stayed sitting on her bed for a moment. What was she doing right now? This was probably a terrible idea. At some point, she won't be able to come back from the recklessness.

"Don't be such a baby. No one will even know you're gone." She said to herself as she stood up and grabbed her bag.

She wasn't going to let Max know it, but she was packing a few duffel bags of her things. She'd keep them concealed with a spell for now. Hopefully, Max didn't get the wrong idea. She wasn't coming over for a booty call or anything. She just needed an escape and a friendly face. A face that was also sick of the world revolving around Brynn.

Just to be safe, she cast an invisibility spell on herself before she left her room. The hall was quiet but she tiptoed around anyway. Once she got to the front door, she went slowly. After a quick peek outside to make sure the coast was clear, she quietly shut the door behind her.

Driving would be a hell of a lot faster, but she was making this journey on foot. Taking one of the cars would be too risky. Although, it might get her the attention that she was missing. Her phone rang right around the time she made it off of the property. It was Max.

"Change your mind?" He asked.

"No."

"What's taking you so long then?"

"I'm walking. Didn't think taking one of their cars was my best choice."

"How far have you made it?"

"Umm, I just stepped off of the property when you called."

She could hear Max sigh and he hung up the phone. What was his problem? She was the one walking, not him. Maybe she should just go home.

All of a sudden, she was lifted off of the ground. She started to scream and her voice felt caught in the back of her throat. She was moving fast. Like, lightning speed. Before she had another second to think, she was being put down in her dad's living room.

"What the hell Max?" she half yelled,

trying to catch her breath.

He shrugged his shoulders. "I'm impatient. And I was sleeping when you called."

"Oh. Sorry. You should have just told me no. Or not answered."

"Nah. I wanted to see you. Why are you here though?" he asked as he closed the door and walked closer to her.

The lights in the house were off and it got extra dark once the door was shut. She got goosebumps when she felt Max's cold draft get close to her.

"Did you just need to get away? Or are you here for something a little more... scandalous?"

Fiona laughed. "I'm not here for a booty call dude."

Her valley girl accent could be cute on occasion. Max always thought it was annoying when he was with Brynn. Without her, he hadn't minded it too much.

"A guy can dream, can't he?" He chuckled as he turned on a lamp. "You miss 100 percent of the chances that you don't take."

"Whatever." She laughed as she rolled her eyes. She flipped her bright hair over her shoulder. "I don't suppose you have any food here anymore?"

"There's some pizza rolls in the freezer. I'll throw them in the microwave for you. If you had given me a head up, I would have cooked for you like I said earlier."

"Have you heard from my dad?"

"Yeah, he sent me a text earlier. There was another attack today."

"Someone needs to do something."

"Like what?" he asked.

"Fight back."

The microwave beeped and Max removed the pizza rolls. He walked into the living room where Fiona was sitting and handed her a plate. She licked her lips and he grinned. She probably didn't even know she did it. It was just a naturally, hungry girl response.

"Let's do it then."

She looked up at him mid bite.

"What? You and me? Together?"

"Why not? The sooner this shit is done the better it will be for everyone. Plus, it would be good for me to get some of this aggression out. What better way to do that then kick some evil fairy ass?"

Fiona smiled as she finished her pizza rolls. She didn't mean to inhale them, but she really was hungry.

"How do we find out where the attacks are going to be? They have been so random."

"When your dad texted me earlier, he said that the suspect was a wood fairy. From what I understand, they smell like a spicy campfire. Surely I can sniff that out. Plus, both attacks have been in pretty isolated locations. I just need to stick to the outskirts."

"Your sense of smell is pretty good now that you're a little vamp."

"Little vamp?" Max asked with an arched eyebrow.

Fiona just laughed her high-pitched, tiny laugh. "Well, I need a little sleep first. Wake me up in a little bit and we can start our stakeout."

She walked down the hall to her old bedroom and flopped down on the bed. She forgot how comfortable it was. She would be asleep in no time.

When Max went to wake her a few hours later, he hesitated before walking into her room. The door was open already. He watched her sleep for a few minutes.

What was he doing? He ran his fingers through his thick hair. He had done his fair share of flirting with her the last two days, but what if she finally reciprocated? How far was he prepared to take things? He wanted to get back at Brynn in so many ways, but there would be no coming back from sleeping with her sister. He rubbed his face before dropping his arms in frustration and walked into her room.

"Wake up, Fi." He said softly as he rubbed her arm.

She opened her eyes slowly.

"Max?" she asked softly, a bit confused. He stared at him blinking a few times before sitting up. "Sorry, I forgot where I was for a minute."

"No worries. You still up for a stakeout?"

"Yeah. Give me a few minutes and I'll be ready."

"I'll get a pot of coffee going and meet you in the kitchen." he said before disappearing.

Fiona rubbed her eyes and flung her legs over the side of the bed. She stretched her arms and let out a big yawn. Maybe if she could stop an attack or at least put up a fight, someone would finally notice her. She hopped to her feet and headed to the kitchen.

Max had two to-go cups sitting on the

counter.

"You like yours extra sweet and creamy, right?"

"Yep. Almost no coffee taste at all." She laughed. Everyone always made fun of how she liked her coffee. "Are you having some too?"

"Yeah. Not as tasty as blood, but caffeine still helps me too. It's weird."

They grabbed their cups and headed out of the house. Max rushed to the car and had the passenger door open before Fiona made it there. Such a gentleman. She hopped in and buckled up.

"Where do we start?" She asked when he got into the driver's seat.

"Well, the way I see it is both attacks have been in isolated areas. We probably need to head to the north end of town."

"Sounds good to me." She said while taking off her shoes.

Max shot her a skeptical look.

"What? If we are gonna be in the car for a while, I might as well get comfortable." She shrugged her shoulders and smiled.

"Just don't put those dirty fairy feet on my dash." He winked as he backed out of the driveway and took off down the street.

Max drove fast. It was a good thing she didn't get carsick.

"Aren't you worried about getting a ticket?"

"My senses are better than you think. I'll know if there is a cop."

She snorted. He could sound so arrogant sometimes. Like a jock, but not a dumb one.

She turned the radio on, found an upbeat pop channel, and put her feet up on the dash just to annoy Max.

He turned the radio down once he turned onto the first dirt road leading to the fairies living out in the boondocks. He rolled the windows down and inhaled deeply. Fiona didn't interrupt. She knew what he was doing.

The first part of the drive was pretty casual. Now that they were in the rural part of town, it was all business. His pace slowed as he glanced in the rear-view mirror. Once he saw that no one was around him, he pulled over to the side of the road. He said nothing but got out of the car.

He stayed right where he stood. He looked around, feeling what direction the wind was blowing from. North. Perfect. He turned in that direction and took a deep breath through his nose. If he picked up on anything, it would most likely be coming from the direction they were heading. He took a few more sniffs and focused.

It was faint, but he smelled smoke. Bingo. He sat back down in the car.

"I think it might be our lucky day." He said to Fiona with a grin. "We aren't close yet, but we are heading in the right direction. Ready yourself beautiful."

"I'm ready." she said plainly.

Max didn't know it, but Fiona had been yearning for this day. She had some angst that she needed to get out too. She wanted to be part of the combat when they attacked the court that day. They made her cast instead. What she wanted didn't matter. She would prove herself today.

They quickly zipped down side roads, zigzagging their way through the country. Max was quite literally following his nose. It was impressive. Fiona couldn't take her eyes off of him. He was laser focused. She could probably take her top off right now and he wouldn't even notice.

The car slowed and Max pulled into a secluded spot. Fiona looked at him for direction.

"We are close. Very close. We need to walk from here."

"Let me cast first. I can make us quiet."

Max nodded and Fiona closed her eyes. She began a soft chant, almost a whisper, using words Max had never heard before. He felt an invisible wave rush over him as Fiona opened her eyes.

"That should do it."

"Wow." Max whispered. "I never felt anything like that when Brynn cast things on me."

"I've always been better than my sister. Let me show you baby." She smiled at him before getting out of the car.

She walked around the car to his side. He nodded in the direction they needed to head. She grabbed his forearm to stop him from walking. She stood on her tip toes to reach his ear.

"You won't think about that Queen Bitch anymore after you see me in action today." She whispered softly.

She released his arm and started walking in the direction he had indicated a moment ago. He didn't have a chance to respond to her. He hoped that she was right, though. Too many of his minutes were still spent thinking about her. He could feel it changing him and he didn't like it.

As they made it to the edge of the woods, a small wooden house came into view. Very secluded.

"Get on my back." Max whispered to Fiona.

Without hesitation, she did as he said and hopped on. She wrapped her arms across his chest and braced for a ride.

Within seconds, they were at the front door of the house. He let her down softly and they crouched beside the front door to listen.

"Make your choice." They heard a voice say.

This was it. There was still time. Fiona cast a shield spell before they made their move. If a fairy threw surprise magic at them, they would at least be protected from the first attack.

On the count of three, they rushed into the house. Just as suspected, magic was immediately headed their way. The shield blocked it long enough for them to charge. There was only one fairy. He was strong, but no match for such a surprise fight. The vampire element was too much to contend with.

Fiona stabbed him in the heart before

Max ripped him apart. The fairy's intended victim was cowering in the corner.

"Are you ok?" Fiona asked the fairy, deploying her wings to hopefully gain a little trust.

Before the fairy could answer, a lion roared as he bounded into the house.

"Wait!" Fiona shouted, throwing up a magical force.

The lion quickly transformed into a man.

"Fiona?" Raef asked, out of breath. "What are you doing out here?"

"Tracking the person behind the fairy killings. What about you?" she said in a snotty tone.

"Trying to find out who hurt your sister." He cut Max a look before turning to leave. He shifted back into a lion and ran back into the woods.

"Weirdo." Fiona snorted as they helped the scared fairy up and explaining what had just happened.

SIX

"Found something." Raef said when Gideon answered the phone.

"Do you want me to meet you somewhere or will you come here?"

"Meet me at my house. I need you *and* the warlock. Can someone else watch Brynn?"

"I can ask Shyan."

"Fine, but no one else in that room but her or Vincent. Not until you two hear what I have to say. Don't trust anyone else."

"Ok. We'll see you soon."

Gideon hung up the phone and sent a text to Shyan asking her to come to Brynn's room. While he waited, he filled Bruce in on the plan. Luckily, he was already there.

Shyan made it surprisingly quickly, rushing in to make sure Brynn was ok. Gideon explained the situation before leaving.

"Please, no one gets in expect for Vincent before we make it back. I don't know all of the details, but if I had to guess I would say there must be a rat."

Shyan nodded. "You have my word."

"Going to get good news, pretty girl." He said quietly in Brynn's ear as he told her goodbye.

He and Bruce were out of the house and on the way in a flash. Neither of them said much on the way. There was no speculation as to what Raef may have found. Just silence and nerves.

When they pulled up the long driveway they could see Raef sitting in a chair on the front porch. He stood up as they came to a stop.

"Thanks for coming so fast, dude." Raef said as Gideon got out of the truck. "Let's go inside to talk. You never know who is listening."

When they got inside, Bruce cast a silencing bubble around the three of them after they got seated. Never bad to err on the side of caution.

There is a small house a few miles from here. A quiet fairy lives there. She's nice. Keeps to herself. I smelled a commotion over there earlier and ran to help. When I got there, the wood fairy I smelled had been killed. However, there were two people I didn't expect to see.

"Who?" Gideon asked, almost afraid to hear the answer.

"Fiona and Max."

"They killed the wood fairy?"

"Yeah. From what it looked like, Fiona must have stabbed him and Max ripped him into pieces. It was a pretty brutal scene."

"So does the wood fairy have something to do with Brynn?"

"No. I have come across two scents while I've been out here. One of them looked me in the eyes today and I have no doubt about it. Max. He has something to do with this."

Gideon gritted his teeth. He should have known. Max was too chicken shit to make a tough decision so he lashed out at a woman. Pathetic.

"And the other smell?" Bruce asked, seemingly on the edge of his seat.

"It's hard to explain. Best I can put together is fresh air mixed with a little bit of electricity and very fresh water."

"How is that even a smell?" Gideon asked his brother.

"Indeed it is my young compadre. It belongs to something so ancient most of you probably haven't heard of its existence. In fact, most who *do* know think they are extinct."

"What?" Gideon and Raef asked in unison.

"That scent belongs to an elemental."

Bruce was right. Neither of them has heard of an elemental. The looks on their faces confirmed that for him.

"They are mystica like the rest of us. They used to be mistaken for shifters which, based on the plainest definition, they are. However, they can only change their shape while exposed to a specific element. That made their existence a difficult one. It was a weakness that was too easy to exploit. As a result, they faded out gradually over time."

"Why would an elemental be connected to this?" Gideon asked.

"I'm not sure. I know how to find out, though. Few people know where to find the elementals. Fortunately for us, I am one of those few. First we need to heal Brynn. After that, we need to take a field trip boys."

Bruce and Gideon thanked Raef for the

information he found. They were in a hurry to get back and heal Brynn. Raef understood.

"Do you already have what you need?" Gideon asked Bruce on their way back.

"I do."

"Thank God. I don't want to wait any longer."

They made a beeline for Brynn's room when they got back. Shyan jumped when the door opened with force.

"You startled me! Any luck?"

"I think so." Gideon said. "As long as Bruce here knows what he's doing."

"This is powerful magic. Both of you should stand closer to the door. I don't know what might happen."

Gideon and Shyan exchanged a look before doing as Bruce suggested.

"This better not hurt her." Gideon said before Bruce got started.

"I assure you, she is in good hands. I

wouldn't risk her life."

With that, Bruce got to work. He retrieved a small bowl from his bag along with some herbs. He unclasped his necklace and removed a chunk of quartz that had been hanging from it. After muddling the herbs with a mortar and pestle, he poured a bright pink liquid into the bowl. After mixing, he added the crystal.

Shyan grabbed Gideon's hand and held it tight. It was hard for both of them to watch. If something went wrong...

Bruce began chanting. It was soft at first. Barely a whisper. As the chant progressed, Bruce's voice grew louder and more aggressive. By the end, he was shouting with such a force the whole room began to tremble. With his last words, he dipped his thumb into the potion and rubbed it on Brynn's forehead. Just like the Lion King.

With a clap of his hands, sparks flew from the bowl and the remnants on her forehead. She sat up and loudly inhaled like she had been suffocating.

"That son of a bitch!" She yelled. "That

son of a bitch did this to me!"

"Max?" Gideon asked as he stepped away from the door.

"Yes." Brynn started to cry, snapping her head in Gideon's direction. "I will make him pay for this."

"I'll be right by your side." Gideon said as he sat down next to her on the bed.

"We will give you two a few minutes alone." Bruce said.

Shyan nodded her head. "We will be back soon."

They closed the door behind themselves and Brynn broke down once they were gone. Gideon sat there with his arms around her. She was so small. She seemed so frail. The fact that she hadn't had anything to eat in such a long time didn't help matters any.

"You have been here every single day. Almost all day. You never gave up. Why not?"

"I made a promise, Brynn. I keep my promises." He scooped up her hand in his.

"Thank you." she said meekly.

"Could you hear any of the things I said to you?"

"I could see and hear everything. I was just trapped inside of myself."

Gideon nodded, thinking about everything he said and did in front of her. Hopefully, there wasn't anything too embarrassing. Surely he would think of something in the middle of thc night as he was trying to fall asleep.

"I love you, Gideon."

"I love you too, sweetheart."

"I know. You ready for some revenge?" She smiled a smile he hadn't seen on her before.

"Oh yeah. I don't give second chances, baby. Especially not when it comes to someone hurting you."

"How did you know how to save me?"

"Long story very short, Raef was at Gwen's place looking for clues. I've had him out there for a while now on a mission. Today, he ran into Max and recognized his scent from Gwen's house. Raef also smelled something else. Luckily knew what the scent was and that was the key to breaking the spell."

"Wow. That's quite a lot to take in."

"Everyone has been working nonstop. I'm not gonna lie to you, it's been a shit show."

"Fairies were attacked?"

"Yes. Several fairies died. Some old court member, a wood fairy, was responsible. I guess word must have gotten out that you were out of commission. It was inevitable. Your mom had been doing her best to keep things going. To be honest though, I think she is struggling."

"What a mess. Do you think the wood fairy was working alone?"

"I don't know."

Before anyone could say anything else, Shyan and Vincent walked into the room.

"You got here fast." Gideon said to Vincent.

"Vampire speed comes in handy from time to time." He walked over to Brynn. "Good to have you back, kiddo." He patted her on the head.

"It's good to be back. Mom, thank you for taking the reins while I was out of commission."

"You're welcome. And thank the stars that you are back. Leading this many people is really not for me. I don't know how you handle it with such grace. I'm glad you get that from your father." Shyan said genuinely.

Brynn chuckled.

"Who did this to you? Who was Gwen helping?" Vincent asked as he took Brynn's hand in his own.

The room was silent for a moment. As mad as they were, neither Brynn nor Gideon wanted to say it to Vincent. Max was his progeny. It was going to hurt.

"Dad, I..." Brynn started to stumble

over her words as she tried to think of what to say. She could feel her face flush. She was a bad liar.

"Just tell me, Brynn. Don't try to sugar coat it."

"Max."

"Damnit." Vincent's voice boomed before disappearing in an instant.

Brynn looked down at the floor. Her dad didn't need this extra drama. Not to mention this was an awful position to be in. His loyalties were going to feel tested.

"Don't worry too much about your father, honey. He will be fine." Shyan said softly, snapping Brynn back to attention.

"Why don't you guys fill me in on everything I missed. I feel like I'm gonna have a lot of making up to do." Brynn said as she stood up and stretched her legs. "And also, I am absolutely starving."

"I already have food on the way." Gideon said immediately.

Brynn shot him a curious look. He shrugged.

"I ordered some of your favorites online. I knew you would be hungry."

She blushed. He took such good care of her while she was spellbound. She was conscious for all of it. Now that she was able to communicate, she was a little nervous. How was she supposed to act around him? It felt like their relationship advanced to another level while she was out of it. Even if it didn't look like it.

Ever since that fated night in the woods, they had been together. It was just kind of understood that there were supposed to be. They felt constantly drawn to each other. It had to be the stars.

She started twirling her hair nervously.

Gideon and Shyan spent the next little while filling Brynn in on all of the details of the recent activities. After the food came, she wanted to keep talking. She sat in the bed, surrounded by her favorite foods. A cheese pizza with extra cheese and lots of parmesan and oregano, chicken lo mein, and a very loaded steak burrito with extra guacamole and queso. She was a happy camper.

"Where has Fiona been during all of this? Is she even here? I haven't heard from her yet."

Shyan was quiet for a moment while she pondered the question.

"I'm not really sure. I haven't seen her today. Maybe not yesterday either. Sorry sweetheart. Things have been very hectic."

"It's ok. I'll call her in a little bit."

Brynn shoved the last bite of lo mein into her mouth. She looked up to see Gideon grinning.

"What? You know how long it's been since I had some food. *And* I could see and smell everything you ate while I was out of it." She said with a mouthful.

"I just didn't know it was possible to be sexy while stuffing your face, but here you are. Killing it."

She laughed as she felt herself turning

beet red.

"I miss being young." Shyan said with a chuckle. "Why don't you take the rest of the day to get readjusted. We can announce your taking back over the reins tomorrow."

"That's probably for the best. I still feel a little out of it."

"I imagine. It will take a bit to get your bearings. Finish eating, go for a walk, whatever you need to do. Call me if you need me."

Shyan walked over and kissed Brynn on her temple like she used to do when she was little before leaving the room.

"What do you wanna do?" Gideon asked before flopping down on the bed next to Brynn. She scrambled to not lose the rest of her food. She smacked his arm and he laughed. It was good to have her back and animated.

"Wanna go for a walk in the woods?"

"I was hoping that's what you'd wanna do. Do you wanna change your clothes? I've been doing my best to dress you, but I don't know if I've done a decent job or not."

"This is fantastic. It's hard to go wrong with yoga pants. Comfortable and functional. She looked down at the black yoga pants and hot pink t-shirt with a big, back Adidas leaf stretched across the center."

She blushed at the thought of him seeing her naked and vulnerable. Better him than a strange nurse or something, but still. Awkward. They weren't in that comfortable phase yet. She still felt self-conscious about everything.

He was a gentleman about it each time. He never stared or copped a feel. She knew he probably wanted to. They were a couple now. It wasn't like he hadn't seen her naked before. It was different though. She got to join in before.

"I'm ready when you are, kitten." Gideon winked.

"I'm ready." She said as she stood up slowly.

She was woozy and slightly unsteady

on her feet. Gideon noticed and grabbed her hand.

"Let's just take it slow. If you need a piggyback ride at any point, just hop on."

She smiled and nodded her head. He popped her on the butt as they walked out of the room. She giggled and leaned into his arm. She inhaled his cinnamon scent and was instantly at ease.

SEVEN

"Hey Fi. It's me. Call me back." Brynn hung up the phone and rolled her eyes.

Where was Fiona? She had called her four times since she woke up. No one knew the last time they saw her. Not even Gideon. She was starting to worry. What if she was in trouble?

"Tell me about the elementals." Brynn said to Gideon once they made it into the woods.

"I don't know much. Just what Bruce has told me. They are an incredibly old race.

Original mystica. They are shifters. Not like me, though. They have to be in their element in order to shift. Apparently, that extra caveat makes it more difficult to shift. As a result, they kind of died off."

"So what, earth, wind, and fire?"

"And water." He nodded.

"Were the elements hereditary or assigned?"

"I'm not exactly sure. My guess would be that it is based on the zodiac. That's just a total guess, though."

"Makes sense."

They slowly walked hand in hand through the woods. Once they made it to a clearing full of bloomed wild flowers, Brynn stopped and sat down to enjoy the fragrance. Gideon picked a flower and tucked it behind Brynn's ear.

"What did Raef say they smelled like?"

"Kinda like a spicy bonfire. Why?"

"I think there was one at Gwen's house.

It was an older woman. She smelled kind of smoky. Something about her felt almost... ethereal. I don't know how else to explain it."

"Did she say anything while she was there?"

"It was hard to hear and a bit hazy. She gave Gwen money and some sort of crystals. She said that I couldn't take my throne. I need to find her, Gideon. I need some answers."

"Bruce can help us. He knows where the last of the elementals stay. He can take us to them."

Brynn nodded with far away eyes. She was deep in thought.

"I wasn't supposed to remember anything. Gwen tried to put a block in my mind. I could feel the magic. For some reason, it didn't work. She doesn't know that though."

"It didn't work because you're the Queen B. That magic knew better, girl."

Brynn laughed. Gideon's twang was so charming. She could listen to it all day long.

"Anyway." She continued, "The elementals are going to have to decide which side they are on. Let's call Bruce and get this going. I want Raef to come with us. My dad, too."

"Raef wouldn't have it any other way."

Gideon made the phone call to Bruce while she laid back and relaxed in the sun. She squeezed her eyes shut, enjoying the warmth on her face. She buried her bare feet into the thick grass and dirt, getting as grounded with the Earth as she could. The breeze blew slightly and the fragrant air swirled around her.

"Bruce said he will call us with a confirmation soon."

"Fantastic." Brynn said with her eyes still closed.

"Where is all of this headed, Brynn? What do you want?"

She chuckled as she thought about the contradiction of what she actually wanted. Peace and revenge. What a duo.

"It's not that easy to answer. I want to live peacefully and freely. But then this other piece of me is just begging for a little revenge."

"I don't see any reason why you can't have both. Eliminate the enemy and then just live happily ever after." Gideon winked at her and laughed.

He laid down beside her and looked up at the clouds. She scooted over and laid her head on his chest. She felt so small surrounded by his muscular arms and chest. They spent a long time not talking and simply enjoying each other's presence. Brynn's stomach started to growl at some point.

"Hungry again?" he asked with a raised eyebrow.

"Yeah. But this time for dessert."

Gideon chuckled.

"Let's go make that happen then."

She smiled as Gideon hopped up and extended his hand to her. She grabbed it and pulled herself up. Once they were back on the road, she was excited to find Gideon pulling into one of the best ice cream shops in the area. Double Scoop was a local legend.

She got a dirt cake sundae and was in absolute heaven for the rest of the ride home. Layers of chocolate cake, cookies and cream ice cream, and whipped cream were packed into a giant cup like a dream. As they were pulling up the driveway, Gideon's phone rang. It was Bruce. The conversation lasted less than a minute. When he hung up, Brynn looked at him waiting for the scoop.

"Bruce said he is about to head our way."

"Perfect." She replied, tipping the cup upside down and getting the last few bites of ice cream out of the cup.

Brynn walked into the closet to find clothes to change in to the second they got into her bedroom. If she was going to meet an elemental, she needed to be dressed for possible combat. Yoga pants just wouldn't do. It was an iffy situation. Gideon walked in behind her. Her heart sped up as he rubbed his hands down her arms.

"You don't stop do you?" he whispered

in her ear as he started to kiss her neck all the way down to her collarbone.

Some leader she was... she already forgot what she was doing. Was that all it took? A kiss from a hot guy? No. It was *this* guy. There was something different about him. Some sort of pull. Maybe it was the stars. Maybe it was more than that.

She dropped the shirt in her hands to the floor and slowly turned around to face Gideon. He smiled.

"I missed you." He pulled her close to him and pressed up against her.

"I missed you, too." She shivered.

There was a knock at the bedroom door.

"That ain't even right." He said in a low growl. "How'd Bruce get here so damn fast?"

Brynn giggled as he walked out of the closet, closing the door behind him. She dressed quickly. She was eager to go.

"Are you sure you are ready for this

today, my lady?" Bruce asked when Brynn walked back into the bedroom.

"I appreciate the concern in your voice, but I'm sure. I need answers, Bruce. If you wanted to cast a little something extra on me, though... I wouldn't say no."

"Say no more." Bruce chuckled before casting something.

She didn't ask what the spell was. Whatever it was already left her feeling more fortified. She felt it start at her toes and travel all the way up her body.

"When will Raef be here?" Brynn asked Gideon as they all moved toward the door.

"He just pulled up." Gideon answered while shoving his phone back in the pocket of his jeans.

"Perfect." She opened the door and led everyone out of the house.

"Your father is coming with us as well." Bruce said as he hurried behind them. Being stout sometimes made him a bit slow. He always said his cat-like agility made up for it.

Brynn nodded. She wanted him to be there. This road could lead to more bad news about Max, though. She didn't want to put him in that position.

"I'll see you when you get home, sweetie." Shyan called out to Brynn as everyone walked out the front door. Her mom wasn't usually like that. It was a little weird. She *had* just been spellbound for a while, though. She needed to keep that in mind. People would probably be trying to handle her with kid gloves for a little while. Until she had a chance to prove herself, at least.

Raef and Vincent were already waiting in Vincent's SUV when they got outside. It was a good choice. They would all fit comfortably in there. It had a third row, so it was pretty roomy on the inside. The window tint was dark, which was always a plus for something like this.

Brynn and Gideon piled into the back with Raef. Bruce rode shotgun.

"You're the navigator *and* the DJ up there Catman. I hope you brought some good jams." Gideon chuckled as they backed out of the driveway.

Bruce drew a map in the air with his finger and it hovered over the dash like some supernatural GPS system. Before anyone in the backseat processed what they just saw, Bruce turned the music on. When DMX started coming through the speakers, everyone in the backseat laughed.

The speakers rang out. "Ya'll gone make me lose my mind, up in here, up in here." Brynn, Gideon, and Raef all sang along.

"I don't think that was is what they were expecting." Vincent laughed as he looked at Bruce.

"You never know when the old man might surprise you. It is always good to keep people on their toes, my friend." Bruce smiled.

As the song ended, things quieted down.

"Now that I have everyone's attention, let's discuss our upcoming moves. The elementals are very private and *very* paranoid. There aren't a lot of them left. They shift like normal shifters if they have their element available. It is important to keep in mind that it does not require much of that element to shift. The flick of a lighter, a bottle of water, a handful of dirt, a small breeze.

You cannot tell by sight what someone's element is. Be on alert at all times. Pay attention to everything. It is unfortunate that it will be dark outside by the time we get there."

"Will we be able to make it to them without being noticed?" Brynn asked.

"Absolutely not. They will know we are there before we get there. There is a reason they are not extinct."

"They won't attack first? Couldn't we be walking into a trap?"

"No. They will wait to see what we do. They won't engage in combat unless they are backed into a corner or are absolutely certain they have quite an upper hand. They aren't big risk takers."

Vincent turned off of the main road and began what looked to be quite a secluded drive in the woods. Everyone believed Bruce, but it was still hard not to worry that they were driving into an ambush.

After a few more turns, they eventually pulled up to an old piece of chain link fence. It was no longer upright or preventing travel onto the property ahead. It was halfway attached to a broken down concrete pillar.

"Let's walk from here." Bruce said quietly and everyone got out of the car.

"You walk up front with me, Brynn. You are the Queen. They will respect your position." Brynn nodded and joined Bruce at the front of the line.

Slowly, they began to walk down a small, overgrown trail. Luckily for them, the moon was bright enough to light their way. Small mimosa trees were lining the trail. Blackberry vines were woven all around them. Everyone's shoes would probably be stained by the time they made it back. It was better than battling thorns at least.

Brynn noticed that they were walking without making a peep. She couldn't even hear Gideon's boots and they were pretty heavy. Bruce must have cast a few things before they got out of the car. Good thinking.

A cool breeze rushed over them and Brynn shivered. They weren't alone.

"State your business." A voice came out of nowhere. Her stomach dropped.

Bruce looked at Brynn and nodded as if to indicate it was her time to shine.

"My name is Brynn Aliger. I am..."

"The new Fairy Queen." The voice cut her off. A small framed woman came into view. It was hard to tell much about her in the moon light.

"And you are?" Brynn asked, trying to sound confident.

"My name is Ecco. I am the leader here."

"I come seeking information."

"Yes. I know why you are here. I have been expecting you. Come. I will give you what you seek."

Ecco turned around and began walking

further down the trail. She had the same vibe as the woman from the woods, but less ethereal. Brynn glanced quickly at Gideon and he gave her a small nod. She turned and began to follow Ecco hoping that she wasn't walking into the lion's den.

Soon the path began to open up and a garden came into view. Ahead in the distance were several large, luxury style homes. They made their way to the largest one in the center.

It was made of brick that had been whitewashed. There were many large panel windows with white frames. It was three stories tall and it looked like most rooms had their own balcony. These people were living better than anyone expected.

Once they neared the front of the house, two men bowed their heads to Ecco before opening the doors. There were several people scattered throughout the house. They all turned to look. No one said a word. Maybe Ecco was who she said she was.

"We can talk privately in my study." Ecco said over her shoulder as they approached a room with an intricate mahogany door. "There is a safety mechanism put in place to prevent anyone outside from sneaking a peak when the door opens."

"What does that mean?" Brynn asked, skeptical of the pseudo disclaimer.

"It will be dark and claustrophobic for a moment. Only until the door latches."

Brynn shot her a doubtful look before nodding her head. There was no point in turning back now. She had already come so far. She was leaving with answers.

Here goes nothing.

EIGHT

The room was dark. Like, can't see in front of you dark. It felt like everyone was packing in like sardines and Brynn was about to worry that they had made a grave mistake. The light didn't turn on until everyone was in the room. Once the door latched and the room lit up, she let out a soft sigh of relief.

Brynn got a good look at Ecco for the first time and was taken by surprise. She looked like a person divided. Fiery red hair on one side and icy white on the other. One golden eye and one blue. Freckles on one side and none on the other. She was beautiful.

Bruce was wrong. You *could* tell what

their element was by looking at them, Brynn thought to herself. Ecco must have been special. She had two elements: fire and water. As Brynn continued to glance around the room, she saw the woman from Gwen's cabin. It was hard not to gasp. She realized why she felt different than Ecco. Her element was wind. Brynn's hair was braided together down one side of her head, but she swore she could feel it blowing around once she saw her.

"I told you I would give you what you wanted." Ecco said with a confident tone. "I have no place for traitors among my people."

"No offense, but why would you consider her a traitor? She tried to harm *my* race, *me*, not yours."

"We have strict rules here. We have to. My race has been dwindling for years. Without order, we would have been completely gone by now. These rules do not allow us to hurt another race, especially when unprovoked. And we certainly *do not* conspire with them. A vampire at that." Ecco scoffed. "No offense to you, sir." She motioned toward Vincent. "You might be a half breed, but you are vampire enough to understand."

"If you cannot conspire, why are we in this room right now?" Brynn tilted her head to the side.

Ecco let out a single laugh.

"Just because we stay concealed does not mean that we are ignorant to what is going on with the mystica around us. You have started something... quite interesting. Fairies always seemed to take the same approach as us. You didn't associate with the other mystica. I guess you could say that I am interested in what you are doing."

"I just realized that maybe we were wrong about the boogeyman. Plus, we are stronger when we work together. More protected."

Ecco made a noise but said no words. Brynn didn't know how to read it.

"You are mystica also. You are welcome to take your place at the table with the others."

"Don't mistake my words. I think it is interesting. I just do not understand your motivation. To me, it seems like a poor choice.

Nevertheless, I think it best to stay on everyone's good side. Greytha forfeited her place here when she broke the rules. If you want her, she is all yours."

Brynn thought for a moment. She wanted answers. She did not want the burden of a prisoner though.

"I would like to speak with her. I do not wish to hold her as my prisoner. What happens to her after I leave is up to you."

"Very well." Ecco said and took a step back out of the way.

"Why?" Brynn asked coldly as she moved to stand in front of Greytha.

"I was out on a hunt in the woods. The vampire found *me*. You could tell he hadn't been a vampire for very long. That's when they are the most volatile. He said the fairy in the woods told him where to find an elemental. She needed a hair for some sort of spell. He said he would follow me home and kill me if I didn't cooperate."

Brynn laughed. She sounded maniacal. Gideon grinned. He knew where this was about to go. He felt it in his tattoo. He waited eagerly for the show. Ecco saw his smile and her curiosity was piqued.

"Wow. *You poor thing.*" Her over the top speech was amusing to her group. "So, you were just taken advantage of. That monster. You must have been so scared." Brynn was beginning to talk fast.

"Y-yes ma'am." Greytha stuttered.

"Do you know what the most interesting thing about this whole 'Fairy Queen' thing has been since this all came about?" she said with exaggerated air quotes.

Greytha shook her head. Brynn smiled.

"The subtle, unseen differences. For example, the block that you and Gwen thought was nestled nicely into my brain. You know, the one that you thought would suppress my memories?"

Greytha's expression turned from innocence to horror in an instant.

"Watch this." Gideon mouthed to Ecco and nodded his head toward Brynn like an excited little boy.

Brynn slapped Greytha in the face.

"I'm sorry ma'am!" she shouted. Her light brown hair clung to her forehead that was undoubtedly covered in sweat.

"I don't want any of your sorries, bitch. I want the truth and I want it now!"

With the last word, her wings popped out and the ground shook beneath them. A single white feather floated through the air, finally coming to rest on Gideon's shoe. He bent down and picked it up and put it in his pocket.

"This is your last chance." Brynn shouted.

The ground remained unsteady and you could see electricity beginning to form at Brynn's fingertips.

"I met him at a bar. You know, one of those place where you can go and make a few bucks off of vampires that want a little bit of strange blood. We go back into one of the rooms for a little privacy, but instead of taking a drink all he did was complain about this 'little slut' that broke his heart. It was so annoying." She rolled her eyes.

The electricity began to quietly hum at the word slut.

"I told him for a few more bucks I could hook him up with a fairy that could probably get him a little revenge. He paid me the money and I made the call. When it was time, he paid me more money to go to the woods and give up some hair. No one would expect an elemental spell. Most people don't even know that we exist. It was a good plan."

"You stupid little tart." Ecco called from across the room. "How dare you betray us! I hereby sentence you to death."

Before she could say another word, Brynn snapped her fingers and all of the electricity that had been building transferred right to Greytha. She screamed loudly, the lights burned out, and silence fell on the room.

All Brynn could hear was her own heavy breaths. After a moment, a row of emergency lights came on, dimly lighting the room. A thin haze of smoke filled the room.

"I told you this place was fortified." Ecco said plainly.

"Thank you for this." Brynn said to her while walking over and extending her hand.

"You handled this differently than expected. I respect your style." Ecco said genuinely.

"If you ever change your mind about joining us, or just having a conversation about it, come talk to me."

"I might see you soon." She shrugged. "One of my guards will see you out."

Ecco hit a button and someone from the outside opened the door. They made their way off of the property and back to the car without saying a word. Once they were loaded up, Vincent got the SUV turned around. As soon as they made it a safe distance away, the silence broke.

"Woo, Brynn. That was some of that Queen B shit I was talking about." Everyone in the car laughed at Raef's comment.

"Thanks for being here guys. All of you." Brynn said thankfully.

"There's nowhere else any of us would be babe." Gideon kissed her on the temple.

"Besides, I've never seen someone get zapped like that before. It was pretty cool, dude." Raef chimed in.

"Well, I'm glad you thought it was cool. I didn't even know it was gonna happen. I was just as surprised as everyone else."

"How did you know to snap your fingers?" Vincent asked.

Brynn shrugged her shoulders. "I just knew. I don't know how to explain it."

"I understand." Vincent replied plainly. She believed that he did. He might be a vampire now, but he had the same linage she did that gave her this responsibility.

"Now what?" Gideon asked.

"Now we find the missing players responsible and make them pay." Vincent answered.

No one said anything else. Everyone knew what he meant. It was going to be painful for him. As Max's maker, he could physically feel what Max felt. The pain of death would be crippling.

Once they pulled back up to the house, Brynn was relieved. She kept telling everyone that she was fine, but she was exhausted. Everyone piled out of the car and she grabbed Gideon's hand before he got too far from her. She was positioned at the end of the seat with her feet on the edge of the door frame.

"Are you staying with me tonight?" She asked him quietly. He turned around to face her.

"I was hoping to." He put a hand on each hip and pulled her closer to him. "I've spent every night with you, watching over you, yearning for you to wake up and snuggle up to me. I'm looking forward to finally having that tonight. To be honest, I don't want to wake up alone ever again. I just want to wake up to you."

She blushed as she smiled and he helped her out of the SUV, sneaking a quick kiss on her neck first..

"Let's make a beeline for the kitchen when we get in there. I am hungry." Gideon declared.

"Why didn't you get food for yourself earlier?"

"Earlier was all about you. I didn't even think about it."

"I'll make you something." She smiled and led him into the house.

She was happy to find that Shyan beat her to the meal and there was food prepared for them already. She didn't actually feel up to cooking. She would've done it though. He had done so much for her.

"I guess you'll have to owe me a rain check." Gideon joked as they sat down and started to eat.

"Where's Fiona?" Brynn asked her mom.

"I'm not sure sweetie. I tried to call her earlier, but she didn't answer."

"Aren't you worried about her?"

"Not really." Shyan shrugged. "She has been isolating herself a lot lately. She is still struggling with the loss of Drake. Everybody grieves their own way."

Brynn nodded and continued to eat. Even if she was depressed, she thought Fiona would be there when she woke up. Maybe not the old Fiona, but they had gotten close before she was attacked.

After all of the food had been eaten, everyone started to excuse themselves from the table.

"Let's stop by Fi's room on our way to ours." Brynn said to Gideon as they walked out of the kitchen. He agreed.

To her disappointment, Fiona wasn't there. She tried to call her, but still no answer. She put her ear up to the door to see if she could hear it ringing. Nothing.

"I'm getting to the bottom of this tomorrow." She declared.

"I'll help you." Gideon said before

opening the bedroom door. "After you." He said as he ushered her in."

"You seem awfully eager." She teased.

"I told you." He said as he picked her up. She wrapped her legs around his waist and locked her feet together. She giggled as he walked over to the bed and tried to toss her onto it. She was locked in place. He grinned a mischievous grin before letting the two of them fall onto the bed. He put a hand on either side of her head and hovered over her.

"I want to snuggle."

"Such a teddy bear." She laughed as she pulled the rubber band out of his blonde wavy hair, letting it fall down around his face.

"You can't tell anyone that." He laughed. "They need to think I am the baddest bear in the woods."

"Your secret is safe with me."

They both laughed. He kissed her on the nose.

"Better be." He winked at her before

pulling the covers back and turning the lamp off.

She inhaled deeply, enjoying the comforting smell of cinnamon. It smelled like home. He laid down on his side and pulled her close. He mumbled something about not being the little spoon.

NINE

Just like Gideon expected, Brynn started her investigation into Fiona's whereabouts as soon as the sun was up. She seized her opportunity at breakfast while everyone was gathered together to find out when anyone last saw her. From the best she could tell, it was when Vincent sent her to his house for supplies. The supplies were delivered, so she had to have made it home with them.

She decided to call her one more time before she took the investigation on the road. She expected the same five rings and then bubbly voice mail. Would she bother leaving another message? Probably. After the third ring this time, someone picked up."

"Hello? Fiona?" Brynn asked after a moment of silence.

"Look who's finally awake."

She felt herself get flushed. Max.

"What have you done with my sister you son of a bitch?"

"Calm your tits, Brynn. Your sister is fine. She's with me now."

"Bullshit. Fiona wouldn't do that to me. Let me talk to her."

"You should have left well enough alone Brynn." Fiona's voice piped up.

Brynn was shocked to hear her voice. She was almost lost for words.

"Is that where you have been? With Max?"

"Like anyone even cares. All any of them have cared about is you. No one even noticed that I was gone." Fiona's tone was snotty and full of attitude.

"Well, I did. *Immediately*. What are you even doing, Fi?"

"What do you think?" she heard Max quietly laughing in the background.

"Really Fiona? I mean, what the hell? Really?"

"Why do you even care Brynn? You slcpt with Gideon almost immediately. It's not like you are sitting around pining over Max or anything."

"You know it wasn't like that Fiona. Besides, some things are just *off limits*. I would *never* have done this to you."

"Because you didn't get the chance to. In case you are forgetting, my boyfriend died because of you."

Brynn was offended. How dare she say such a thing?

"That's not true, Fiona. You can't trust Max. He is the reason I was spellbound!"

"I know that. He told me everything."

Fiona laughed rudely.

"Why are you doing this, Fiona?"

"Oh no! Does this displease the Queen? What penance shall I pay for these atrocities?" Fiona was laughing hysterically by the end of her sarcastic comments.

Before Brynn had a chance to hit her back with something, the line was dead. She was seething. She had been so worried about Fiona. So mad that no one was concerned about where she was. All of that just to be stabbed in the back.

"Well, I wasn't expecting that." Gideon said, finally breaking the silence.

"Is she right? Did people notice she was missing?"

"I don't know. I was so consumed with you that it was hard to notice much else. You know how much time I spent in this room with you. If I had to guess, she is probably right. She could have felt forgotten, but she should have understood the circumstances. Your sister is pretty immature."

"Ugh. How can she be so short sighted?" Brynn said feeling dumbfounded.

"What do you want to do about it?" Gideon asked her.

She thought about it for a moment.

"Nothing. I can't do anything about it. If it isn't her decision, it will only make things worse."

"You're probably right. Maybe it will work itself out anyway. Max's days are numbered after the stunt he pulled. Soon he will be a non-factor."

"You're right. I didn't think about it like that."

"That's why we make a good team."

"I can't let this keep me distracted. Could you call a meeting? I need to talk to everyone now that I'm no longer spellbound."

"You got it."

"ASAP."

"Consider it done."

"Do you think we can get word to Ecco about the meeting as well? I'd like her to have the opportunity to be part of it."

"I'll send Raef out there. He won't mind. He's a very curious person. Another trip out there will be right up his alley."

"Thank you. Hopefully she will take me up on it."

"Anything else you need me to take care of?"

"I'd really like to see Quyen. I miss her. We have so much to talk about."

"She's already expecting us for dinner tonight."

"You're great." She beamed.

He laughed. He was thankful that she appreciated him being so on top of things. Truth be told, being her mate was the reason. It wasn't like this for him in the past. He wasn't a bad boyfriend by any means, but the doting on, the provocativeness, the instincts... those were all mate things and it was all new to him.

Now wasn't the time for such a conversation, though. Fairies didn't have mates as far as he knew. It was going to be difficult to explain. He needed more time to piece the conversation together. So, he pulled out his phone and got to work on the meeting.

While Gideon was otherwise occupied, Brynn went looking for her parents. She could call them, but something about wandering around the house seemed more peaceful. She found her mom in the library.

"Hey, pumpkin." She said when she saw Brynn walk in. She was sitting in one of the large, black leather chairs with a thin green book in her hands.

"Hey mom. Have you seen dad? I wanted to try a little sparring now that I am rested. I wasn't sure if he would be up for it or not."

"You mean if he's not too preoccupied with the situation with Max?" Shyan asked. She always had a knack for knowing what part of the story Brynn was leaving out.

"Yes ma'am." She said softly.

"Sweetie, Vincent will never put anything before you. Sparring with you would probably bring a smile to his face. He's probably outside in the garden."

"The garden?"

"Yeah. He's been trying to do a little yoga out there every day."

Brynn looked shocked. "Yoga?"

"Don't tell anybody." Shyan laughed and waved her hand in the air. "He's already pretty embarrassed to even be doing it. It took a lot of convincing to get him to try it. I think it will be good for him, though. He's always so uptight."

"I won't say anything." She said with a smile as she left the room. Her dad doing yoga. What a funny mental picture.

She walked out the French doors leading to the back yard and made her way to the garden. It was a beautiful part of the property. It was surrounded by tall hedges. Once inside, the landscape was adorned with hydrangeas, wildflowers, and fruit trees. In the center of it all was a two-tiered fountain.

You could sit on the nearby benches and watch the birds bathe in the fountain stream. It was a very peaceful place.

"Killer downward dog." Brynn yelled across the garden once she saw Vincent, almost making him fall. He stood up quickly and brushed himself off. He shook his head.

"I suppose I have your mother to blame for this. It was her idea after all."

"Don't be mad at mom. I asked her where I could find you. Plus, she might be right. This could be good for you."

"What's up then Queenie?" He stood up and stretched.

She laughed.

"Do you think we could spar a bit? I'm afraid I'll be a bit rusty from lack of movement while I was out of commission."

"Absolutely. I'm always down for a good sparring session. What do you want the ground rules to be?"

"Wings out. But just a little bit of

vampire speed. I need to work my way up to it."

"You got it."

And just like that, it was on. Brynn was right, she was a little rusty. Her timing was off and she was slow. No matter how hard she tried, Vincent kept getting the upper hand. It pissed her off. She tried to harness that anger and make a move, but it didn't work out.

"Focus." Vincent said after pinning her for the fourth time.

"I'm trying." She said, frustrated.

She exhaled and tried to shake it off. This time she tried juking around him and catching him from behind. He saw her coming a mile away. When she tried to make her moves, he grabbed her arm and took her down again.

"What has a hold on your mind right now?" Vincent asked, pausing to catch his breath.

She didn't want to say it out loud. It was too much. The rotten cherry on top of the spoiled sundae for both of them.

She tried once again to catch him off guard, but he took her down with little effort.

"Tell ya what, kid. You can either take me down or tell me about it. Those are your two options. The choice is yours. Fight back like I taught you." His voice was stern.

She dug her heels into the ground and pushed as hard as she could. She jumped in the air and swung her leg, but he caught it and threw her aside like a ragdoll. She slid into the hydrangeas. She sat in the dirt for a moment, contemplating her next move. Vincent walked over to her and extended his hand. She grabbed it and stood up.

"Go on with it, then." Vincent said once she was on her feet. She stood silently for a moment, contemplating what to say to him.

"Fiona is sleeping with Max!" She finally snapped and burst into tears.

"She's what?" his voice boomed. "This has gone too far."

Brynn continued to cry and Vincent

put his wing around her shoulders.

"I hate that I'm crying over this." She rolled her eyes as she wiped the tears from her cheeks.

"Sometimes you just need to get it out. Max was your first love and a pivotal part of your life. It's understandable."

"Dad, I don't care about who Max sleeps with. My sister, though? AND she was dumb enough to fall for it. I feel like a fool. That's why I'm crying. Don't be mistaken. These are angry tears."

"Let's go inside. It's time to finish this once and for all."

Brynn didn't say a word. She quietly followed Vincent back to the house. She didn't know what he had planned, but she could tell that he was serious. He stopped and looked back at her right before they walked into the house.

"I want all of us together for this. Grab Gideon and bring him to my study. I'll get your mother."

Brynn nodded and they made their way back into the house. She last saw Gideon in the kitchen, so she headed there first. Nothing. The library was empty too. She peeked through the front door to make sure that his truck was still there. The last place to check was the bedroom. He didn't usually spend time in there during the day. Except when she was comatose.

"Are you in there, Gid?" She called out as she was getting close.

"Yeah." He called back to her.

She walked into the room to find him hard at work. He had laid out an outfit for her. She assumed it was for the meeting that she asked him to organize.

"The meeting is scheduled for tomorrow at seven. Raef is currently on his way to the elemental compound, and I pulled this outfit out of the closet for you. I thought you might like to wear it for the meeting."

She knew that she was in a hurry, but she had to stop for a second to admire him. He went above and beyond for her every day. Even when she was spellbound, he didn't stop. How lucky was she?

"Thank you." She stammered. "The outfit is perfect. My dad wants us to meet him in his study."

"Is everything okay?"

"Ehh. I was trying to spar with dad. I fought like trash. It was awful. Anyway, he kept pressing me about what was on my mind and I told him about Max and Fiona. He got pissed and said he wants the four of us together in the study. I don't know what he's got going on."

"Alright. Let's get at it then."

He grabbed her hand when they made it out of the bedroom and held it in his. She was so powerful, yet so small. Fierce and fragile all at the same time. Her shiny brown hair was succumbing to humidity. It was wavy and thick with tiny baby hairs sticking out. He loved it.

"You're looking at me like you're hungry." Brynn said through a series of giggles.

"You have no idea." He winked at her and she blushed. Her stomach was flooded with butterflies.

TEN

Vincent's study was empty when Brynn and Gideon arrived. They sat down together on a cushioned bench. He held her hand in his and couldn't ignore the soft hum coming from his tattoo.

"Do you feel that too?" he leaned over and asked Brynn.

"The vibration? Yeah, I feel it. I can hear it also."

"Yeah, me too. I wonder what it means."

"I don't know. It feels kind of comforting." She said calmly.

"Yeah, it's kinda givin' me the warm

and fuzzies too." He nudged her with his elbow and chuckled. The blue t-shirt he was wearing clung tightly to his biceps. It caught her eye.

"Good! You kids are already here." Vincent almost shouted when he walked into the room. Brynn jumped in her seat, making Gideon snicker.

"What's goin' on boss?" Gideon asked Vincent.

"I've given Max a chance to come to me on his own. I didn't want to force it. Unfortunately, he refuses to be a man about things. So now, I *have* to force it. I can use my maker bond with him to compel him. He will have to show up here to me."

"That's why you wanted us to be together." Gideon noted.

"Exactly. Bruce and Madeleine are outside waiting. This is the safest option."

"What do you have to do, dad?" Brynn asked quietly.

"It's all in the blood. I have to put some

of my own blood into a conductive vessel. Then, I have to focus all of my energy into calling out to Max. Once I reach him, I demand that he show himself to me. He won't have a choice."

"Will it hurt?"

"It's gonna zap my energy, but no. It will not hurt anyone."

Vincent sat down at his desk and placed a small copper bowl engraved with silver symbols down in front of him. Shyan walked behind the desk to join him. She placed a small, shiny dagger next to the bowl. She quietly cast something under her breath.

"Let's get started." Vincent said calmly as he picked up the dagger.

He slid it across his left palm and held his hand over the bowl. A small stream of blood poured out into the vessel. When he was done, Shyan quickly wrapped a piece of cloth around his hand before sitting down in the chair next to Brynn. Vincent picked up the bowl and held it in his hands. He stared into the bowl as if he were in a trance.

Everyone sat silently on the edge of their seat, not knowing what to expect. After a moment, Vincent shoved the bowl away from him and leaned back in his chair.

"It's useless. He has me blocked."

"He can do that?" Brynn asked, surprised.

"It isn't easy to do. Someone must be helping him. Maybe a witch or a warlock. He couldn't do it on his own."

"Perhaps it is Gwen." Shyan suggested.

"What's your next move?" Gideon asked.

"I don't know. I would prefer to confront the situation here rather than on his turf. Even if it is technically still my turf also. It'd be hard to know what I was walking into."

"Would your maker be any help?"

"Maybe. I don't know. I try not to call on him if I can help it. Things are complicated."

Gideon wanted to ask why, but he

figured it would be best if he didn't.

"How many fairy vampires do you know of?" Vincent winked. "Talk about being the black sheep, ya know?"

Gideon nodded and grinned.

"Way to read the room, Vincent."

"I'd be curious too, man. I get it." Vincent stood up. "We are expecting guests tomorrow. Let's get through the meeting and then figure out our next move."

"Good idea." Brynn piped up. "This meeting will be a good way to gauge how much on my side people really are."

"True. Once we know that, we can formulate a more accurate plan."

Shyan excused herself to go start cooking. Everyone else left when she did.

"Have you heard anything from Raef?" Brynn asked Gideon once they weren't within earshot of anyone else. If Ecco did show up, she wanted it to be a surprise to everyone. It would be easier to explain at one time.

"Yeah. He sent me a text a few minutes ago."

"And?"

"I'll just read it to you in my best Raef voice." Gideon smirked.

He did the hang ten sign with his fingers before clearing his throat. Brynn laughed.

"Dude. I think this girl likes me. I invited her over to get to know a fellow shifter, but she told me no. Something about rules. She's playing hard to get. I bet she shifts into something playful. Anyway, she said she would think about the meeting. Can I come for dinner in case she shows up? It could be like a chance encounter. Could be fun."

Brynn laughed hard.

"Your cowboy surfer guy is great."

"Hey now. He's the weird one for not having a southern accent. He grew up the same as me. We should sound the same."

"Well, my sister sounds like a valley

girl." Brynn shrugged. "It happens."

When they made it back to the bedroom, Brynn flopped down on the bed.

"What's on your agenda for the rest of the day?" Gideon asked as he shut the bedroom door.

"Nothing until dinner tonight. Did you have something in mind?"

"I thought you and I might both benefit from some more time in the woods."

"That sounds wonderful. I need to put my feet in the dirt and feel a little more grounded."

"Great. I have a lunch packed for us already. We just need to grab it out of the fridge on our way out."

Brynn laughed.

"Of course you packed a lunch."

Gideon winked at her. If she only knew how many things that he *didn't* do. He tried to keep the doting to a minimum. Even if it did go against his mate instincts.

He wanted to have that conversation with her so badly. To confess his love... explain what the bond meant. The timing just wasn't right. There was too much going on. Maybe he was just being selfish, but he didn't want any preoccupations competing for their time. When the time came, he just wanted their focus to be on them.

Damn, he felt like such a sissy for having those thoughts. Someone was gonna revoke his man card soon if he didn't get it together.

"Are we going to come back before we go to Quyen's house?"

"It's up to you. I'm good either way."

"I'll just wear something that I won't need to change out of. Give me just a minute."

Brynn disappeared into the closet. Gideon took the opportunity to grab a few of Brynn's things and put them in his backpack. A hair tie, lip balm, gum... all things she would verbally regret not grabbing before leaving the house. She might have been a fairy queen, but she was scatter brained.

After a few minutes she emerged from the closet, dressed in a pretty floral dress.

"Don't worry." Brynn exclaimed before lifting the front of her dress up.

"It has built-in shorts. It's an all-purpose kinda dress."

"Yes ma'am I suppose it is." Gideon laughed as Brynn grabbed her bag. "You nearly gave me a heart attack though when you pulled that skirt up. I thought you were about to show me something else."

Brynn could feel her face turn beet red.

"I'm ready when you are." She somehow managed to squeak out. Ugh. She felt so nervous around him now.

"Let's go then, darlin." He opened the bedroom door for her.

They made their way through the house, stopping in the kitchen to grab their lunch.

"Are we walking or driving?" Brynn asked once they made it outside.

"Both I guess, I have a spot in mind. Let's drive part of the way. There is a good place to park and walk."

Brynn nodded and hopped in Gideon's truck. She was excited about their outing. Things were different now. She didn't know if he felt it too, but she had a hunch that he did. There was something unspoken between them. There had always been chemistry there. Something bigger than usual.

"Hang on tight." Gideon said, interrupting Brynn's thoughts before taking the truck off-road.

So many girls would hate this, but Gideon saw Brynn's little grin as the ride turned bumpy. She liked it. There was an edge to her that most fairies were missing. He was crazy about it.

He punched the gas a little. Brynn laughed when it knocked her back in her seat.

"We're parking right up there." Gideon said, pointing to a shady area under tree cover.

"Nice and secluded. I like it."

Gideon slowed the truck and parked. Brynn quickly opened her door and hopped out. She had already taken her shoes off. She inhaled deeply, enjoying the smell of the woods. There really was nothing like it.

"Do all fairies like the woods like you do?" Gideon asked as he came around the truck to meet her.

"Yes and no. I'm sure it's the same for shifters. We feel connected to the earth. Some of us like to stay more in tune with it than others. I love planting my feet in the dirt and grounding. I think it cleanses us. Then you have my sister, who would prefer to make up dance routines in her bedroom."

Gideon pulled his shirt off and threw it into the truck through the window that was still rolled down. Brynn could feel the pit of her stomach drop. She was instantly nervous. Those tattoos. The abs. All of it.

"You ready?" Gideon asked as he turned back around.

"Ready." She replied, keeping the other thoughts to herself.

He grabbed her hand and led her into the woods. There wasn't much of a path, but she could tell he had been there before. He seemed to know exactly where he was going.

The scent of wild jasmine filled the air. Everything was so lush. Late spring in the south was a magical time of year. The smells were divine and everything was blooming and beautiful.

"It smells amazing today, doesn't it?" He tilted his head back and inhaled deeply.

"It does. Hard to beat the smell of jasmine."

"You got that right."

As they made their way deeper into the woods, Brynn began to hear the soft trickle of water somewhere in the distance. She was unfamiliar with this part of the woods. It was far enough away from her house that it would have been off limits for her before the prophecy talk began. This new freedom she found herself having was exciting.

"We're almost there." Gideon whispered in Brynn's ear.

She was instantly covered in goosebumps. It sounded crazy, but Gideon could tell. He felt her energy. She was nervous, but in a good way. As the water came into view Brynn smiled.

"I thought I heard water." She chimed.

"Have you ever been out here?"

She shook her head.

"I didn't think you had. That's why I wanted to bring you here. I knew you would like it. Plus, it is close to Quyen's house. When we are ready to head her way, she's just on the other side of those Magnolia trees up there." He pointed to the north.

"This is perfect." Brynn said as she found a soft patch of grass to sit down on. Gideon took a seat beside her.

There were so many things that she wanted to say, but she was scared. She didn't like feeling vulnerable and after the whole spellbound ordeal, it was a hard feeling to avoid. When she was little and felt too scared to do something, she would tell herself "three, two, one, go" and just do it. She did that now quickly in her head before blurting out the first thing that came to mind.

"What's going on with us? I know you feel it too. What is it? Just the stars? Residual energy from that night?"

He clammed up for a moment. This was the last thing he expected her to bring up. Playing it aloof seemed so disingenuous. He couldn't do that to her.

"Yeah, I feel it too."

She was expecting him to say a little more, but nothing came next.

"You're holding something back."

"Yeah. I just... well... it's hard to explain."

Brynn was offended. Hurt, really. Maybe she was wrong about it all. Maybe it was all because she had been spellbound. Merely something she had been building upon her head but shouldn't have been.

"It's fine Gideon. Let's just forget about it."

Her disappointment flooded him. Shit. This wasn't how he wanted any of this to go.

"Don't feel disappointed, Brynn."

She looked at him, surprised that he picked up on her emotions like that. Her fists were clenched, desperately trying to stave off the tears she felt forming in the corners of her eyes.

"Yeah, I can tell you feel that way. Look, I think what we are feeling is more than just the stars." He threw his hands down as if to give up. "Brynn... you're my mate."

ELEVEN

Everything was hazy when Brynn opened her eyes and looked around.

"Brynn, are you ok?"

She suddenly realized that Gideon was staring down at her which meant she must be laying down. She blinked a few times and glanced around her.

"What happened?" she asked, confused.

"You fainted."

She continued to lay there in the grass for a moment before everything came back to her. Gideon told her that she was his mate. How could that be? She wasn't a shifter. Fairies didn't even have mates like some of the others did. She felt a bond too, though. One that she couldn't explain.

Gideon stuck his arm out and helped Brynn sit up.

"Well, this has been kind of a disaster." He said as she got her bearings.

"What do you mean?"

Gideon sighed.

"I have been trying to figure out how and when to have this conversation with you. I was trying to wait until you had less on your plate. I know that fairies don't have mates like we do. It seemed like a difficult thing to explain. I certainly never expected the news to make you faint." He ran his hand through his hair. What a catastrophe.

"You're right. Fairies don't have mates. But I feel a bond with you. Like a kind of... pull I guess. Like magnets. Being away from you feels wrong somehow."

"I might have said something sooner if I knew you felt the bond as well. I didn't think you could, but what you described was pretty spot on. I mean, why do you think I have been Mr. Johnny-on-the-spot? And you've been getting the watered down, she doesn't know she's my mate version."

She smiled and he leaned in to kiss her. All of this time taking care of her while she was spellbound, all of the wanting to act like a mate but not being able to... it all came to a head when his lips touched hers. He felt his soul ignite.

She could hear him growl softly as he kissed her neck. Her tattoo was pulsating.

"Do you want to be my mate?" Gideon whispered in her ear. "If you say yes, that means you're mine. Forever. The bond will be sealed and even if we both wanted to, we couldn't undo it."

She knew all of that. Even though fairies didn't have mates, she still knew what it meant and how it all worked. He was right. The bond was permanent. Stars would seal the deal immediately once the words were spoken. It wasn't like a silly human marriage. They could change their minds at any time. This was often the biggest decision of a mystica's life.

It could be a risk, but she knew what she felt. God wouldn't let the stars mislead her. She was still part angel, after all.

She looked into Gideon's hazel eyes. They almost seemed to be shinning. Her tattoo continued vibrating out of control.

"Yes, Gideon. I do want to be your mate."

He reached down and kissed her. She felt lightheaded again and worried that she was going to faint. Then she realized the intense pain that she felt behind her ear. In a flash it was gone. Gideon must have felt it too because they both stopped kissing.

"Did you feel that?" Gideon asked her.

"Behind your ear?" She replied.

"Yeah. Let me take a look at you."

Brynn turned her head and Gideon brushed the hair away from her neck. He chuckled for a moment.

"What?"

"Look behind my ear and I'm sure you will see."

He tilted his head down and she took a peek.

"Another tattoo. I really should have guessed. Are those runes?"

"That's what it looks like to me."

"Do you know what they mean?" She asked, still examining his new mark.

"No. I know who might, though."

"Quyen."

"Yes ma'am." He laughed.

Gideon got to his feet and turned around to help Brynn up.

"My Queen." He said as he extended his hand.

"I guess that makes you my king now, huh?"

He just laughed as he pulled her up off the ground. She brushed her dress off and wrapped her arms around him. He buried his nose in her brown, braided hair and inhaled deeply. She was finally his. He pulled her tightly to him before releasing her.

"Want a piggyback ride to Quyen's house?"

"I can't say no to that!" she exclaimed as she quickly turned around and jumped on his back.

He walked them through the thicket of magnolia trees. As promised, when the land began to clear, Quyen's house came into view. She walked out onto the front porch when they got close.

"I guess congratulations are in order." Quyen shouted once they were within earshot.

"How could you possibly know that?" Gideon called back to her.

"Because more of the prophecy has

been revealed."

"I hope that's a good thing." Brynn sighed in Gideon's ear. Her arms were still around his neck.

"Don't let her fool you. She knew we were mates before I even told her."

"Must be nice to have all of that insider information!" Brynn giggled.

Even without the prophecy, Quyen would have known something was up. Gideon couldn't wipe the grin off of his face. He wanted Brynn from the moment he first laid eyes on her at Vincent's house. Now she was his mate. She was his and he wanted the entire world to know. He couldn't lie... he wanted that weasel Max to know too. He won.

"You better calm that Alpha energy down babe." Brynn laughed.

"I can't help it." He said as he got to Quyen's steps. Brynn hopped down and gave Quyen a hug.

"I missed you girly! I'm glad you are back among the living." Quyen said as she hugged Brynn. "Come in. We have a lot to talk about."

"It has been a busy day." Quyen called out behind her as they walked into the house. Gideon closed the door behind them and they followed Quyen to the kitchen. "Dinner is almost done."

"Thanks for having us over for dinner, cuz." Gideon said as he pulled a dining room chair out for Brynn.

"So let me see here..." Quyen started as she scrambled around the kitchen. She took the lid off of a big pot and started stirring. "The two of you are mates. Even though fairies don't have mates. And I've never heard of any type of cross-species mate before. Am I right so far?"

Brynn nodded.

"Anything else?"

"Yeah." Brynn pipped up. "When I said yes to being Gideon's mate, we were both gifted with new tattoos again."

"Let me see!" Quyen almost dropped

the spoon on the floor she turned around so quickly.

They both turned their heads so she could take a look.

"Runes. That's unexpected."

"Do you know what they represent?" Gideon asked. "You are the only person I know who might be able to read them."

"Well, they are the same on both of you. Not surprising. It's old. Like old, old. I'm sure I can translate it, though. I just have to find the right book."

She scurried back to her pot. She dipped the spoon back in and took a small taste.

"Dinner is almost done and then I will get down to the bottom of it. And by the way Brynn, welcome to the family. I already knew you would be part of it, but of course I couldn't say anything."

"Ya know, things could be a lot easier if you could just drop hints on occasion." Brynn grinned.

"You know I can't!" Quyen laughed. "Trust me, I want to all the time. When you were spellbound and I could talk to Gid, I wanted to tell him about the good things on the horizon so bad. I said more than I should have once and I was so worried that I ruined everything."

"That changed everything for me, Q. Those few words gave me all the hope I needed to see it through. You don't even know." I'm glad the stars weren't mad about it.

"Good. Don't get used to it." She winked and grabbed dishes out of the cabinet beside her.

She loaded three plates with linguine, delicious meat sauce, and lots of Parmesan cheese.

"Dinner is served." She said as she brought plates to the table.

Things were relatively silent as everyone ate. Quyen was a good cook. The sauce was her grandmother's recipe and had been simmering all day. The pasta was homemade.

"I could get used to eating like this." Brynn said and she put her hand on her belly. "I am stuffed."

"Raef and I were lucky that Quyen knew how to cook. She has kept us fed all these years."

"Well, we were all lucky that grandmother wrote her recipes down. She was a good teacher."

After everyone was done eating, they retired to the living room to get more comfortable. Quyen grabbed a few books out of the cabinet and brought them into the room with them.

"There are old runes in these books. Maybe we can find the symbols in here and figure out what they mean."

The books looked heavy and very old. Brynn wondered how old they must be. They were leather bound with some sort of gold script on the spine not written in English. The three of them sat on the couch together flipping through the pages.

As usual, page after page of

disappointment preceded any good news at all. Luckily, it didn't last too long before something looked familiar. They all saw it at once.

"That's it!" Brynn exclaimed.

There they were, both symbols on the same page.

"What does it say, Quyen?" Gideon asked.

Quyen studied it for a moment and then looked at the tattoos.

"It's a binding rune. The extra marks represent loyalty, love, life... and death. This is very permanent, you guys."

Brynn and Gideon both nodded almost in sync. It was nothing they didn't already know.

"I guess that brings us to the prophecy. *And* now that you are mates, I can tell you at the same time. You are considered to be one flesh. Brynn, in the past I could tell you new prophecy information but not Gideon. You would get the first word. I have been anxiously waiting for this day. I knew it was coming soon. I only know so much, though. Timing is the hardest thing to figure out.

Anyway, when you reach certain milestones along the journey, more of the prophecy is revealed to me. I myself am still in the dark about a lot of things. It's just the nature of the beast I suppose. Before the two of you got here today, I had a vision. When I checked the scroll, more words were there."

Quyen got up and walked to the bookshelf on the other side of the room. She grabbed a hidden rolled up parchment and returned to Gideon and Brynn. She cleared her throat before unrolling the scroll.

"When the cure is found and the stars align, the bond will be sealed. Nothing can sever the tie. Including death.

There will be a fracture. A rift will open and an enemy will arise. Righteousness will meet evil. The wheels in motion will not stop.

Balance needs to be restored to prevent extinction."

"Cryptic as always." Brynn commented

and smiled at Quyen. "Can you tell us about your vision?"

Quyen hesitated.

"I don't know. I'm afraid if I do, it might influence your decisions. I don't want to tempt fate."

"Can you give us anything, Q?" Gideon piped up.

Quyen thought silently for a moment.

"Be careful. Just because someone was an ally or friend before, doesn't mean that they will always be. Sometimes a person's hurt can turn them into a sour person. You never know what someone is hiding."

Brynn nodded. She understood. Quyen had to be talking about Max. She hurt him. She knew then the risk that she was taking. Once he heard the news about Gideon being her mate, things would probably get worse. Hell, he had already tried to hurt her via Gwen. Who knew what he would do next.

Gideon could feel the anxiety building in Brynn. He reached down and gave her hand a squeeze. She felt so petite in his grasp. He knew why she was worried about Max. He was too. Brynn relaxed when she felt his touch. They tried to push the worries out of their minds and just enjoy the rest of their evening.

After they left, Quyen went outside and sat down on her porch swing. Anxiety swirled around in her chest. Being the holder of the prophecy was an arduous task. The vision she had earlier kept playing out before her eyes. Battle. Bloodshed. Death. She couldn't talk to anyone about what she saw. It all stayed bottled up inside. She wiped her eyes and took a steady breath.

The path could always change.

TWELVE

"How worried should we be about this Max situation?" Shyan asked as she brushed her hair.

Vincent sighed. He sat on the edge of the bed tying his shoes. He rubbed his hand on his face.

"I don't know. It's not good. He wants to kill one of our daughters. The other one has run away with him. He is volatile... and dangerous. Young vampires are the strongest. And he has a *big* chip on his shoulder. I've seen the way Gideon looks at Brynn. Max isn't going to be able to handle what is coming."

"Yes, I have seen that look. I don't envy our girl, Vince. She has the weight of our world on her shoulders and she is barely an adult. The fate of our race is quite a hefty responsibility. Have you heard from Fiona at all?"

"No."

"It might be time to call on Gautier." She said quietly.

"We will see how tonight goes. I might not have to."

Shyan started to speak but there was a knock at the door. Vincent walked over to open it. He was surprised to see Brynn standing there.

"Good morning, sweetheart." Vincent said with a smile. "Come on in."

Brynn walked in and sat down on the bed.

"Any idea about a head count for tonight?" she asked as she stretched out.

Shyan walked over and sat down next

to Brynn. She grabbed a piece of her hair and began to braid it.

"Around ten. Are you nervous?" Shyan replied.

"Kind of. More anxious than anything. I'm ready to get past a few things."

"I know you are, sweetie. So tell me, what's going on with you? I see the new marks behind your ear."

"It looks like some sort of binding rune to me." Vincent spoke up.

Brynn was surprised to hear her father say that. It took the three of them a lot of research last night to figure it out. Vincent knew right away. She could feel all eyes on her.

"You're right. It's a binding rune. We found out what it was last night. It was a gift from the stars I suppose."

"We? You and Gideon?"

"Yeah. He has the same mark on him. Quyen helped us figure out what it all meant."

"Why would the stars mark you with a binding rune?"

"Because I think God has a sense of humor." She laughed nervously and hesitated for a second. "It turns out, I am Gideon's mate."

No one said a word. They just stared at her hesitantly. Neither of them was surprised.

"Something has felt... off, I guess, since I regained my cognition. Yesterday, Gideon told me that I was his mate and it explained everything. I know it doesn't make a lot of sense and I don't know how to explain it. Once I said yes to him, we were marked."

"Brynn, do you understand how permanent this is?" Vincent said in a tone that suggested he was worried about his daughter.

"Yes dad, I do. After it happened, we went to Quyen's house. More of the prophecy was revealed. It says that not even death can break the bond. Truthfully, I knew that in my heart before I even said yes to him. I would make the same decision right now if given a second chance."

Truth be told, neither Vincent nor Shyan were surprised. They saw the way Gideon looked at her... the way he doted on her... it made sense. It did worry them, though. This sort of thing was unheard of. There were no cross-species mates. Leave it to Brynn to break that rule.

"Anyway, I just wanted a head count. I am running through things in my head. I want to be prepared. I'd ask you to keep the mate thing to yourselves for now, but I have a feeling it will be too obvious anyway."

"It will be fine, honey. Tell Gideon we would like to speak with him at some point."

Brynn nodded and headed back to her room. That went better than she was expecting. She thought they would at least seem surprised. It was a controversial topic.

The rest of her afternoon was a blur. Between prepping for the meeting and worrying about what to do with Fiona, her brain was stuck between burnt out and overdrive.

"Raef will be here in an hour." Gideon said, breaking her out of her own thoughts.

Her stomach fluttered.

She was nervous about tonight. She hoped people would take her seriously. Yes, she was young. That didn't mean that she was weak, though. She had what it took. Hopefully, everyone would see that.

She slipped on the dress that Gideon picked out for her. He made a desirable choice. It was a flattering cut and it made her feel glamorous. It was deep blue with a semi plunging neckline. The cap sleeves made it playful;, but the long length kept it business appropriate.

"You're gonna command the whole room in that dress." Gideon admired.

Brynn blushed.

"Does it look ok?" She twirled from side to side.

"Girl, it is taking everything in me not to take it right off of you and throw you onto this bed." She shook her head and laughed as she put on the finishing touches.

As soon as she was ready, they both

headed toward the front of the house. Brynn wanted to be there to welcome her guests as they arrived. Vincent told her earlier in the day that there would be a couple of people that she didn't know. A new vampire and warlock.

The agreement was to have two representatives from each race at the meeting. Vincent didn't want to call on Gautier, so he phoned a friend instead. Bruce called on a fellow warlock to join him as well. Brynn still hadn't told anyone about Ecco.

She paced nervously in the entryway until people began to arrive.

"Wooooo!" Raef hollered when he walked in the front door. Quyen followed closely behind him. "Looking good sister-in-law."

"Raef. Dude what did I say about discretion?" Gideon rolled his eyes.

"Heck bro, I'm sorry. I'm just excited, ya know?"

"I know. I know. I am too. You can head to the kitchen if you want to. There is a plate of food ready for you."

Raef smiled as he walked past them toward the kitchen. Quyen gave them a wink as she walked by. The wolves were the next to arrive.

Daveson and Finn both seemed happy to see Brynn. She hadn't seen either of them since the battle. They were dressed casually in jeans and button up shirts. They looked like the Vikings that were taught about in her history classes in human school. They proved to be good allies before. Hopefully, she would be able to say the same thing at the end of the day. After a few pleasantries were exchanged, they headed to the study.

When Bruce showed up, he had a small framed man with him.

"Brynn, I would like to introduce you to Hector. He is my oldest friend in the warlock world. He is someone worthy of trust."

"It's a pleasure." Brynn said as Hector took her hand and kissed it. He had dark tan skin and a pencil thin mustache. He had the same catlike eyes as Bruce. "Please make yourself welcome in the study."

As they walked away, Gideon jabbed Brynn with his elbow.

"That suit is amazing!" He whispered loudly.

He wasn't wrong. It was a mustard yellow suit made out of what looked like velour. The blue silk shirt underneath stood out against the brightness of the suit. The paisley tie brought the entire ensemble together. It was straight out of a 1970's sitcom. Brynn chuckled and smacked his arm.

"Brynn." Vincent said from around the corner. He appeared in a flash with another vampire. "This is Jacques."

"Mademoiselle." Jacques said to Brynn as he took her hand. "It is a pleasure to meet you."

His accent was thick. He sounded like he came all the way from France. Vincent quickly escorted him toward the study. Based on the way Jacques was looking all around him in wonder, Brynn didn't think he spent much time in America.

Madeleine and Shyan soon emerged from the kitchen.

"We saved Quyen. Raef had her hostage in the kitchen talking about some dream girl he met recently."

Quyen giggled and Brynn rolled her eyes. She knew Raef wouldn't be able to keep his mouth shut. Gideon rubbed his temple. Brynn thought he looked so cute. The charcoal grey suit he was wearing fit him well. The purple shirt he wore complemented his hazel eyes. His hair was pulled back and you could see his new rune mark. Brynn liked it. It was meant for her just as her mark was meant for him.

"We will get everyone situated. Come in when you're ready." Shyan said before turning to leave.

Brynn just stood there in silence for a moment. She didn't know what her next move was. As Raef emerged from the kitchen, it all fell into place.

"Raef." Brynn said sternly, catching his attention immediately. "I need you to wait here by the door in case Ecco shows up. If she does, and I am serious when I say this, bring her directly to the study. *Do not* stop to flirt. You can do that afterward."

"You got it little sis." Raef gave her two thumbs up.

Gideon stuck his elbow out and Brynn grabbed the crook of it with her hand. They made their way to the study. He opened the door for her and everyone stopped talking when she walked into the room. She and Gideon made it to their seats and she began talking.

"I'd like to thank everyone for coming this evening. I'd also like to thank my mother, Shyan, for filling in for me when I was ill. I'm sure most of you know, I was spellbound. Thanks to the help of Bruce, I am able to talk to you all again. I have come to discover that Max was the one behind the attack. A witch named Gwen helped him. The magic they used was able to be obtained through a race some might not even know exists... an elemental."

Gasps traveled around the room.

"I heard that elementals were a myth."

Finn spoke up from across the room.

"I can assure you we are certainly not a myth."

Brynn jerked her head to the side as she heard a voice at the door. Ecco appeared almost on cue. She had another elemental with her. Raef came running up behind her.

"She's fast." He gasped. "I'm sorry, Brynn."

"It's fine, Raef. Thank you."

He nodded and left, closing the door behind him.

"Hello everyone. My name is Ecco. This is Roi." She motioned to her left. "Thank you for the invitation, Brynn. As you know, this goes against our rules. However, new times call for new approaches. You have our attention."

Gideon grabbed two more chairs and brought them over to Ecco and Roi. Their presence made Brynn feel empowered. Everyone in the room kept trying to sneak peeks at them. It was understandable.

Especially Ecco.

"That timing worked out well, but I assure you it wasn't planned. I met Ecco recently in an effort to track down those responsible for my illness. Her leadership impressed me. I invited her to this meeting, but I didn't expect her to show up.

I want us all to work together and be a united front against those who wish to fracture our world. Some of our former court members have been lashing out at other fairies. I have heard whispers that everyone else is dealing with treachery of their own. I want to suggest that we help each other eradicate the threats. It would be a move that our enemies would not see coming. A threat to any of you is a threat to me. I hope that you can feel the same. We can make sure our world is safe and protected, but we *must* work together."

Everyone whispered quietly amongst themselves for a few moments. Brynn sat quietly, giving them time to make a decision. The wolves were the first to speak up.

"You saved several of our family

members that were being held prisoner by the court. Our pack will forever be indebted to you. You can count on us."

Brynn began to feel a bit of relief. One ally checked off the list.

"I obviously have a vested interest in this." Vincent began. "Jacques, what do you think?"

"It is true that vampires and other mystica, fairies especially, do not have an excellent track record. However, times are changing. If you believe in this cause, Vincent, then you have the full support of the brood." His accent was thick but everyone got the gist of what he was saying.

"The shifters are obviously on board." Gideon said with a grin.

Bruce and Hector both voiced their "warlocks are on board" message in unison.

All eyes turned to Ecco.

"What do you think? Can we form an alliance? It works both ways. You will get our protection now as well."

"We have a deal... at least for now."

Brynn shook her hand and addressed the room one last time before dismissing everyone. She was planning on walking Ecco and Rio out, but Raef beat her to the punch. She shouldn't have been surprised.

"I know you are probably gonna shoot me down, but I'm gonna ask anyway. If you ever want to go for a run in the woods some time, let me know. I don't know what you shift into but if you're anything like me, that urge to run can't be beat." They overheard Raef ask Ecco once they made it to the front porch.

"Maybe." She shrugged before giving Raef a wink and hopping into the passenger seat of the bright blue Lexus she arrived in. Rio was in the driver seat. Raef grinned as she pulled away.

"I'll take it. A maybe's not a turn down." He said out loud to himself.

THIRTEEN

A few days had passed since the meeting and things had been pretty quiet. Nervousness stirred within Brynn. There was a full moon on the rise. It wasn't just any full moon, either. This was a special moon. Humans called it a "super moon." In the mystica world, it was called a "vision moon." It typically happened once per year. Some considered it to be the most important moon of the year.

For the wolves, it marked the time for survival quests, where maturing pups go out on their own for a season. Those who survive are free to find or start their own pack. Some don't make it back. They say it separates the weak from the strong.

For many other mystica, it was a time for reset and reflection. It made Gideon want to go to the woods and run. In fact, he and Raef couldn't stop talking about it. She agreed to go with them, but she wasn't doing any running. She was looking to lounge and star gaze.

In past years, Brynn would find a nice secluded, grassy patch on the property to disappear in. She tried to become as one with the earth as she could. She would reflect on life and try to do her best to honor the tradition. She was looking forward to being in the woods for the occasion this year. A first for her.

Shyan cooked a protein packed dinner for everyone in preparation of the evening. Roast with gravy, sweet potatoes, bone broth soup filled with tiny meatballs, and green beans with bacon. She even premade trays of finger foods for anyone who felt the need for some late-night snacking.

After dinner, Brynn and Gideon

excused themselves to go get better dressed for the evening. Brynn put on black leggings and a tank top that had plenty of room for her wings. Gideon picket out a white t-shirt and joggers. Easy clothes to take off, according to him.

"We should bring a plate of dinner over to Quyen's house while we are out there." Gideon suggested as they walked out of the bedroom.

The plan was for Gideon and Brynn to meet Raef in the woods by the water. Quyen was feeling under the weather, so she was sitting this one out. Brynn would sit by the water and watch their clothes until they got back. If she got bored, she could always cut through to Quyen's house. It seemed like a pretty good plan. She was excited to just be out, soaking up the moon's energy. This was always such a magical night.

The drive to the woods was quiet. They left the radio off and had the windows down. It was a nice evening. The humidity was low and it felt close to 72 degrees. There was a slight breeze. Cool, but not enough to give a chill. The crickets chirped and the frogs croaked, almost in harmony with each other. Gideon's demeanor was giddy as they got close to their destination.

"You're cute when you're excited." Brynn joked as she watched him from the passenger seat. His hair was pulled back, but it was still flying wildly in the wind. She had opted for two French braids. It was low maintenance and so far, holding up well.

Gideon slowed the truck as he pulled off of the trail. They had finally made it. He took his shirt off as soon as he got out of the truck and threw it into the cab.

"Don't worry. I'll keep my pants on for now." Gideon laughed as he walked around to Brynn's side. He took her hand in his and began leading her into the woods. The moon was so bright they didn't need flashlights. Even without the moon Gideon could find his way to the creek. He had been this way so many times.

Once they reached the water, Raef appeared.

"Hey bro and little sis. You ready to run, dude?" He clapped his hands together and Brynn couldn't help but laugh at the excitement.

Gideon pulled her into his arms and gave her a hug. He kissed her and twirled one of her braids around his finger.

"Let me know if you need me." He said as he pulled her as close as he could.

"Can you still hear me when you shift?"

"Babe, I couldn't miss it if I wanted to." You are in my brain no matter where I am or what I'm doing.

"Have fun running around out there. Love you."

"I love you, sugar."

He pulled off his joggers, threw them at Brynn, and turned into a bear in a flash. He took off in the woods, getting the drop on Raef.

"Cheater!" Raef yelled before shifting and taking off after him.

Brynn chuckled and walked over to the creek bank. She put their clothes in her bag and set it down. She found a soft spot and sat down. She sank her feet into the thick grass, letting cool strands slide between her toes. The moon was high and the way it shined on the water felt tranquil.

She let her wings out and relaxed. This was a good place to reflect. Despite the peace, she thought about Fiona. She missed the version of her sister that she had gotten to know. Did that person even exist or was it merely a character Fiona was portraying? It was difficult to say.

Anxiety hitched in her chest. It wasn't just her thoughts bringing it on she quickly realized. Gideon. She was feeling what he felt. Something was wrong.

Her mate instinct was pushing her to find him. She jumped up and spun around to head further into the woods. She gasped once she saw what was waiting in front of her. Her runes began to get hot. It felt like it was searing her skin.

"You about to fly off somewhere?" Max laughed as Brynn just stared at him.

"What have you done?" Brynn asked,

her fists clenched and ready to fight.

He cocked his head to the side. The slimy smirk on his face made her skin crawl.

"What makes you think I have done something?" His cocky tone repulsed her.

"Because Gideon is in trouble."

"How could you possibly know that?"

"Because he is my mate!" she shouted.

For a second, he thought he felt the ground shake. He tried to remain calm, but he was failing. He opened his mouth. Not to say anything, but because his fangs were about to come out. Rage pumped through his cold veins.

"Did you say that you are his fucking MATE?" he vociferated.

Before she could answer, Max was lunging at her. She dodged him, turning around quickly. She knew he would try it again.

"Too slow." He snarled before grabbing her. "I knew I couldn't trust that piece of trash shifter around you. Maybe I should get a taste of that sweet fairy blood again." He pressed his face into the nape of her neck and inhaled sharply.

Brynn did as her father trained her to do in the very beginning of her training. She dropped her weight to escape his grasp. Before he had time to react, she knocked his legs out from under him with her wings.

"Where's my sister?" she asked between gasps before running away from him.

He stood up and brushed himself off.

"I wasn't dumb enough to bring her here." He scoffed. "Why would I risk my pet?"

"Your pet?" she screamed before charging at him.

Her fury was too much to contain. She knocked Max to the ground. He hit the dirt hard and slid back. He wasn't mistaken earlier. The ground was definitely shaking now.

"How are you doing this?" he yelled, trying to hide his surprise.

"What makes you think I am doing something?" she said in a cocky tone, mocking him.

Truth be told, she didn't know. Surely it wasn't her. Before she could say a word, Max used his speed to his advantage and disappeared within seconds. Once he was gone, Gideon and Raef appeared. He had to have known they were close.

The ground still shook, but the intensity was beginning to lessen.

"What happened?" Gideon asked as he took Brynn into his arms and looked her over.

"Max showed up."

"He did this to you?" He couldn't hide the anger in his voice. He was going to hurt Max for this.

"Yes, after I told him I was your mate."

"I mean, I wanted him to find out but not like this. Not when you could get hurt."

"I'm fine, Gid. He called my sister his pet. I just lost it. I went at him and the ground just started shaking. He thought it was me doing it and took off right before you guys showed up."

"Chicken shit." He said under his breath.

"You were in trouble too. I could feel it before Max showed up. What happened?"

"A couple of wolves. Tweakers. Max probably found them in the woods and recruited them. They will do anything for a little dope. Easy to take out, but still unexpected."

"I'm glad you are okay." She put her head on his chest. He kissed the top of her head. There were leaves and bits of dirt in her hair.

"I hate to break up the moment guys, but we should probably go check on Quyen."

Raef was right. Who knew what Max had up his sleeve. She could be in danger. Raef shifted back into lion form and ran ahead. Brynn jumped on Gideon's back like before. He took bigger strides than her and she was carrying a load already. It just made sense.

Brynn cast a forcefield around them so it would be easier to get through the lines of Magnolia trees. It never felt good to get hit in the face with those thick leaves.

"Thanks, darlin'." Gideon shouted once he realized she cast the spell. He started running at full speed.

Once they got to the clearing, they could see Raef and Quyen standing on the front porch.

"She's fine!" Raef shouted.

Gideon's pace slowed and Brynn hopped down.

"Thanks for the ride, cowboy." She said as she slapped Gideon's butt and laughed.

"We brought you food." Gideon announced once they were within earshot. "How are you feeling?"

Quyen shrugged.

"I'll be alright." She said finally. "What about you?" she looked at Brynn.

"I'm fine. Max showed up." Brynn shrugged.

"And the tremors?"

"Yeah, he took off right after that."

"Because he was scared of you?"

"He thought I was the one making it shake."

"He was right. You were. Angel power to the rescue."

Brynn stared at Quyen for a moment with a look of disbelief. She wasn't expecting a confirmation.

"Haven't you noticed all of the shooting stars tonight?"

Brynn shook her head and looked up into the sky. Star gazing had been her original plan tonight. With all of the excitement, she never got started. Quyen was right though. She had never seen so many shooting stars in one night sky.

"It started after the shaking. Something is starting.

"There will be a fracture." Brynn said quietly. "It was in the prophecy."

"A rift will open and an enemy will arise." Quyen recited in response.

"Those stars are getting bigger." Gideon said, eyes fixed on the sky.

He was right. Slowly the shooting stars were getting bigger and bigger. Brynn stepped closer to Gideon and grabbed his hand. She didn't know what was happening, but it filled her with anxiety. Their tattoos began to pulsate once their hands were connected. Slowly at first, but the pace quickened.

"Gid?" Brynn asked with a panicked tone.

"Just stay calm, Brynn. The starts won't hurt us."

He squeezed her hand tight and it felt like the pulsating was coming to a pinnacle. Suddenly a big, bright light shot across the sky so close that the force almost blew them back. Thunder rolled through the air when it made impact.

"That had to be close." Raef spoke up after a moment.

"It was." Quyen agreed.

"Should we go find it?" Raef asked, hoping everyone would be on board.

"What say you, Queen?" Gideon asked Brynn.

"Let's see what we can find. Q? You up for it?"

"What the heck." She replied as they made their way off of the porch.

"You know, this would be faster if we shifted." Raef suggested.

"Brynn can't shift, Raef." Quyen said with a tone that screamed 'you idiot.'

"Unless she wants to ride a bear." He replied proudly.

"Don't talk about our bedroom plans." Gideon replied casually, sending everyone into intense laughter.

"GIDEON!" Brynn exclaimed while

socking him in the arm. She could feel her face turn a bright shade of crimson.

"What about it, though? You ever rode a bear through the woods?"

She shook her head timidly. "I guess there's a first time for everything."

"Sweet!" Raef shouted as he lost his pants in a hurry.

Everyone followed suit and piled their clothes in Brynn's backpack and began to shift. Gideon shot Brynn a wink before shifting into a bear and walking over to her. He crouched down so she could reach. She used her fairy gifts to give herself an extra boost and she hopped on. She got seated and nestled herself into his fur.

They bounded toward the woods and Brynn held on tight. She cast another forcefield spell on the group and sunk her head down into Gideon's fur. He was warm. She inhaled deeply and thought about how comfortable this felt. How natural.

Even as a bear, he smelled like cinnamon.

FOURTEEN

When they could see smoke, they stopped moving. Brynn hopped down off of Gideon and the three of them shifted back into their human form. Brynn pulled their clothes out of her backpack and handed them out.

"It should be on the other side of the water over there." Gideon pointed.

"That's right where I was when the shaking started." Brynn noticed.

They carefully began making their way to ground zero.

"Did the pulsating stop for you once the star hit?" Brynn asked Gideon quietly enough that Raef and Quyen couldn't hear her.

"Yeah. You too?"

"Yeah. What do you think it means?"

"Your guess is as good as mine, sugar."

"Do you guys smell that?" Raef asked once they were almost to their destination.

Everyone took a moment to sniff the air around them.

"That's not good." Gideon said under his breath.

By the time they got there, most of the smoke had dissipated. The only remnants were slowly flowing out of a massive hole in the ground. It had a diameter of about 6 feet and it looked deep. As they carefully peered over the side, no one could see a thing. It seemed like there was no end in sight to that hole. Everyone expected to see a glowing star at the bottom, but they were met with only stinky darkness. They all took a step back to regroup.

"It definitely smells like sulfur." Gideon said, rubbing the stubble on his face.

"You don't think?" Brynn looked at him. He shrugged.

"You wanna call your dad?"

"Yeah. That's probably a good idea."

Brynn pulled her phone out of her pocket and dialed Vincent. Predictably, he answered on the first ring.

"Hey. Everything ok?"

"It's hard to explain, but do you have time to come to the woods? We are to the west of the compound by a creek."

"The place with all the Magnolias?"

"Yeah!" She was surprised he knew what she was talking about.

"I'll be right there."

Brynn hung up and sighed. She hadn't said anything about Max. Once Vincent got to the woods, she wouldn't be able to hide it. Max didn't beat her up or anything, but you could tell she had been in a tussle. There was no way Vincent would overlook it.

Gideon knew it too. He wasn't looking forward to it. He knew that Vincent would be unhappy with him. He was Brynn's mate and he left her vulnerable. There was no excuse.

"That son of a bitch!" Vincent yelled as soon as he made it to them, which was faster than anyone expected. "Where were you? It is your job to protect her!"

"I know. You're right." Gideon hung his head.

"Dad, wait. Gideon and Raef were being attacked. They had no idea that I was going to be in danger."

"No, Brynn. Your dad is right. You are my responsibility. You are my mate. It doesn't matter where I was or what I was doing, you should have been safe."

"How did you know so fast? You hadn't even looked at me?" Brynn asked Vincent who was still seething.

"I can smell him. You must have made

him bleed."

"Yeah, a little maybe. He ran away before I could tell. That makes me sound like more of a bad ass than I am. The truth is a long story, though."

"In the meantime." Gideon interrupted, "we need you to look at this." He motioned to the hole.

Vincent walked over to the hole and looked at it. He smelled that air. He bent down and touched his fingertips to the edge of the hole.

"This is not good at all. Brynn, cast whatever spell you know to keep anything from coming out of that hole. I'll be right back."

He left abruptly. Brynn had been so focused physical combat lately. Her spell casting was slow. She cast a reverse forcefield on the hole. Hopefully, it would keep everything at bay. She cast some protection on herself and the group as well. It needed something more than she was capable of casting.

Vincent was back just as quickly as he left. This time, Shyan was with him. She immediately began casting more spells on the hole. Everyone stood back and watched her work. Brynn recognized a few things that Shyan was casting, but most of it was new to her. Vincent helped her cast as best he could. To say he was rusty was an understatement.

There was no visible activity at the hole. After Vincent and Shyan seemed satisfied, they approached the rest of the group.

"Quyen, I know what you can say is limited. Does the prophecy speak of this?" Shyan asked as she started looking over Brynn, noticing that her disheveled appearance was too extreme to be because of a shooting star.

"It's true that I cannot say much about the prophecy if it hasn't already been revealed to Brynn. That being said, I can confirm that I have been gifted no knowledge of this hole.

"The newest part of the prophecy said that there would be a fracture. Like a rift that is significant. I think this is the start of something." Brynn told her mom.

"We definitely need to monitor this place." Vincent began to talk but was interrupted by his phone ringing.

"Luther." He said when he answered.

He was quiet for a moment. His body was still as he stood and listened. Whoever this Luther was had a lot to say. Based on Vincent's body language, it wasn't a good phone call.

"Shit" Vincent said as he hung up. "I've gotta go. A coven house was attacked."

Shyan nodded. "Please be careful. It could be a trap for you."

"Don't worry. I'll be smart. Check in soon." He kissed her on the cheek before disappearing.

Another attack. It was all starting to play out. Hopefully, everyone from the meeting communicated with their tribes and spread the word. This was a test. Everyone would show their true colors by the end of it.

Brynn picked a leaf out of her braid and walked over to the hole to take one last look. Shyan followed her over and stood beside her.

"Who did that to your face? Max?"

"Yeah." Brynn sighed. "He ruins everything."

"He's bitter, sweetheart. What did you expect? You broke his heart."

Brynn opened her mouth to protest, but Shyan cut her off.

"The reason why is irrelevant. What's done is done, but it might make things easier if you really think about his motivation. Does he know about your bond with Gideon?"

"He does now. That's what brought this to a head. Well, that and something he said about Fiona."

"She wasn't here, was she?"

"No."

"Like I said, what's done is done. We need to always keep moving forward in life."

Shyan put her arm around Brynn. They stood in silence for a moment, just looking and the shooting stars in the sky.

"Do you mind giving me a lift home? I'm not quite as fast as your father." Shyan laughed.

"Of course. Fair warning, though. These woods aren't the easiest to get through. The shifters can shift and have a fairly easy time with it. Not so simple for us, I guess."

"Isn't it? Let's just fly." Shyan shrugged her shoulders as if she was surprised that Brynn hadn't thought of that.

"I mean, I can get small and glide. Like that?"

"No. Ugh, I have failed you. You really don't know this one? I could have sworn I taught you."

Brynn just shook her head.

"Ok then. Repeat after me."

Shyan recited a spell Brynn had never heard before. She felt a force run through her body. Almost like a buoyancy. She was about to ask her mom what she was supposed to do, but she felt the instincts. She already knew how to fly.

"Damn girl. You been holding out on us?" Gideon joked once he realized what was going on.

"Nah. She just wanted to see what it would be like to ride a bear through the woods." Raef joked and everyone laughed.

"Very funny. Now come on, give me your clothes and let's get out of these woods for the night." Brynn stuck her hands out and one by one they removed and handed her their clothes.

They took off through the trees headed toward Quyen's house. Brynn glided between trees. The breeze blew through her hair and she couldn't help but keep looking around in wonder. She was gonna have so much fun with this when it was a less intense time.

Once they got to Quyen's house, Shyan suggested that everyone stay the night at the fairy compound. With so much going on, it was the safest option. She ran inside to grab a bag of her things. Just some clothes and a few important books, including the prophecy scroll. Once she was back outside, everyone piled into her car. She offered to take them to Gideon's truck.

Shyan opted to ride with Raef and Quyen once they made it to the truck. Quyen's car was a lot roomier. Once Brynn and Gideon were alone in the truck, they both breathed a sigh of relief. They didn't want to say it in front of everyone else, but the stars had been putting them through the ringer.

"This has been intense." Brynn finally said quietly.

"Yes ma'am, it has. How are your tattoos feeling?"

"They have all finally settled down. How about yours?"

"Same. I thought it was gonna explode when that star came shooting through. I don't know how or why, but this is all connected to us somehow."

Gideon put the truck in gear and started heading toward the fairy compound.

He drove slower than usual. Brynn knew it was on purpose. She was fine with it. What she really wanted was to go home and go directly to her room and get in bed with Gideon. She wanted to snuggle until she fell asleep. Well, maybe that and a little more.

She stretched and put her bare feet up on the dash. The wind blew through the open windows. She closed her eyes and enjoyed the feel of it hitting her face. It was supposed to be a nice night in the woods. Too bad nothing ever went as planned.

As they pulled up the driveway, they could see everyone standing outside around the house. They were all looking up and pointing to the sky. The shooting stars were still going strong.

Everyone congregated in the kitchen once they got inside. Thank God Shyan made snacks earlier in the day. They were coming in handy more than she expected them to. She pulled out her phone to call and check in with Vincent after they finished eating. To her surprise, she could hear Vincent's ring tone. He had just walked in the door.

"We're in the kitchen." Shyan shouted.

Vincent made his way into the kitchen and sat down at the table. Everyone had questions but waited to ask any of them.

"Four vampires are dead." He began. "It sounds like shifters are behind it. Gideon, Raef, Quyen... I'm gonna need your help figuring out who the suspects are. I brought some still shots from the surveillance footage."

The three of them walked over to Vincent as he pulled out his phone.

"There were two guys. One had a scraggly brown ponytail that was braided. He was wearing camp fatigues. His accomplice was dressed in a white wife beater and jeans. It looked like they must have shifted and gotten past the checkpoints as animals. A dog and a raven."

"I know those guys. Dwayne and Carl. Complete trash. They usually camp in the woods behind the Big Pumpin' gas station on the edge of town." Raef spoke up.

"I trust you boys can handle this?" Vincent replied.

"We got it, boss. No worries." Gideon assured him.

"Raef, Quyen... glad to see that the two of you are staying here tonight. It is the safest bet. It sure seems that the mystica world has lost its mind this evening I'm afraid."

"That's for sure. I'm afraid there are dark days ahead of us."

The room was quiet. Everyone wondered if that was just a feeling or if she had seen something in the prophecy. Either way, they were all on edge.

FIFTEEN

The sun was barely up when Gideon started making phone calls. He tried to be as quiet as possible to not wake Brynn. The wolves should be up by now. They were early risers by nature. The wolves that attacked him and Raef might have been dead, but he still needed to get to the bottom of it.

"Hey Gid. What's up man?" Daveson's voice was raspy when he answered the phone as if he had pulled an all nighter.

"You sound like shit, Dave. Ya'll have some sort of howl at the moon party last night or something?"

"Yeah, I wish." He sighed. "It was a rough night. Vamps attacked a pack during all that crazy shit with the stars. Bastards ripped them to shreds. I've never seen anything like it."

"Damn dude. I'm calling you about a similar situation. How many did you lose?"

"We've got five dead brothers. It's a tough pill to swallow, man. All pretty young, healthy guys. One just found his mate recently. I don't know why those blood suckers decided to mess with us. We stay away from them. I thought it was mutual. Anyway, did you get hit too?"

"Yeah. Me and Raef in the woods last night. Two wolves. A couple of tweakers. Little younger than middle aged, kinda hippy lookin'. Any ideas?"

"Sounds like Thad and Darius. They'd do anything for a hit. It wouldn't surprise me. I assume you dispatched them?"

"Yes sir. We did"

"Damn dude. Everyone lost their minds last night."

"Yeah. It sounds like it. I'll tell Vincent about the attack on your pack. Expect a phone call from him. Ya'll stay safe out there, friend."

"Thanks, man. You too. Let me know if you run into any more unruly wolves." Daveson started yelling at someone as he hung up the phone.

Gideon sighed as he dropped his phone down on the bed.

"This is a disaster." Brynn said, startling Gideon. He should have known she would wake up. Even if he had been quiet enough, she didn't want to miss out on anything. She probably listened to the entire phone call.

She leaned back on the bed and sighed. The tension in the mystica world was building. Even without the phone calls she would know that. She could feel it in her soul.

"Do you think that hole is going to be significant? I can feel it." Gideon asked as he leaned back on the bed and put his head on the pillow next to Brynn. She leaned her head up against his.

"Yeah, I do. And I can feel it too. I just can't figure out how. We need to do some research."

"I look forward to the day that we can just stay in bed all day and enjoy each other without interruptions. No attacks. No spells. No drama. Just me and you... naked and intertwined."

He started to roll over onto her and his phone vibrated. She laughed.

"I look forward to that day too. Unfortunately, I don't think today is that day." She kissed him on the shoulder.

He grabbed his phone and looked at the screen. It was a text from Raef. He and Quyen had already left for the day. The text said that after he took Quyen home, he caught up with Dwayne and Carl. They were tied up in the car. He was getting ready to take them to Vincent. Gideon was relieved. One less thing to have on his agenda today. He had a feeling it was going to be pretty booked.

"We should grab some food before we start getting too busy." Gideon suggested as he stood up and grabbed his jeans off of the closet doorknob.

Brynn watched him quietly as he zipped he jeans. She wanted to roll around in bed with him all day just as bad as he wanted to. She just didn't talk about it like he did. He smiled when he caught her staring. He struck a pose and she realized she was busted. She let out a loud laugh.

She appreciated his ability to distract her from the drama surrounding her. He opened the closet door and grabbed a few things for her. He tossed them onto the bed.

"Thanks, babe." She said as she grabbed a t-shirt and yoga pants from the pile.

Once they were both dressed, they headed to the kitchen. Even if Shyan didn't make breakfast, there were always scones, danishes, and fruit to enjoy. One thing for sure, no one on that compound ever went hungry.

When they walked into the kitchen, they were happy to see a tray full of various fruit pastries and a plate of breakfast meat. Brynn grabbed a raspberry cream cheese danish and a few sausage links. Gideon piled up on all of the meats... ham, sausage links and patties, bacon, and steak along with a triple berry bear claw. Brynn laughed at the choice. How fitting.

Bruce waltzed into the kitchen about the time that they sat down.

"Good morning, you two. I hope you are feeling sufficiently rested."

"Glad you made it through the craziness of last night, Catman."

"It was an interesting phenomenon indeed." Bruce replied.

"I have so many questions, Bruce. I don't even know where to begin to go for answers. My gut tells me that the answers were given before mine and Gideon's time. We just have to find it somehow."

"Perhaps you should take a trip to the Hall of Records. They will surely have the answers you seek."

Gideon and Brynn looked at each other.

"I thought that place was made up." Gideon said to Bruce in a skeptical tone.

"It most certainly is real, I assure you. Although, it is typically a difficult trek to make if you do not have help."

"What do you mean?" Brynn asked.

"You know how it is with old magic, old spells, old information, old anything... people like to keep it sacred and under lock and key. This is no different. The more people doubt its existence, the safer it remains."

Brynn and Gideon nodded. That made sense.

"How do we get there?" Brynn sounded more determined with each question that she asked.

"You typically have to travel through the Forbidden Forest and then the outskirts of the farthest realm. You follow the water's edge until you reach an island. However, if you have a warlock friend such as me, you portal to the island within a mile of the hall."

"Look, we all know Brynn is already on

board. I think we need a lot more information. How treacherous is this place really? It sounds like it's not really the kind of place you waltz up to and ring the bell. Surely they aren't there waiting for strangers to show up demanding answers."

"Once inside the hall, it is very safe. Nothing to worry about. The trip between the portal and the hall... well, that's a little trickier. It is meant to mislead you and keep you from completing your journey. You need to keep that in mind."

"So what? We have to fight our way there?"

"Just do not venture off. Stick to the mission. There will be many distractions along the way. Don't trust any of them. I cannot stress this enough."

"What do you think?" Brynn asked, turning to Gideon.

"I think your dad is gonna have my ass if this goes sideways." He rubbed the stubble on his face, hating the position he was currently in. "Catman, could this place actually help us? Level with me here."

"Yes. The Hall holds many records and resources that could answer your questions. Although, it is not a guarantee. There *is* a chance that you could get there and be turned away. I have a hunch that they will deem you both worthy, though. After all, there is a prophecy centered around Brynn. The odds not being in her favor are highly unlikely."

"You have a good point. Brynn does seem to have some favor with the stars. Hell, let's do it." Gideon gave in and Brynn's face lit up.

"I will meet you in your room in ten minutes. Make sure you have everything you need to bring with you. Once you get through the portal, you can't get back until you reach the Hall and they send you back."

That little caveat didn't faze Brynn. She was ready for some answers. She grabbed Gideon's hand and led him to their bedroom. She quickly packed her backpack before strapping on several holsters for her weapons. Gideon eyeballed her.

"You expecting battle when we get there?" Gideon asked as he strapped up his combat boots.

"Doesn't hurt to be prepared for all possibilities." Brynn shrugged.

"Are you sure you wanna do this right now?"

"Yes. I have to do something Gideon and I think it has to be something extreme."

"Are you gonna tell you mom and dad where you are going?"

"We."

"Yeah, yeah. Answer the question."

"I was gonna let Bruce tell mom."

"I hope you're ready for that battle when we get back. Then we get there and get back. We do what Bruce said. I don't care what comes up, we ignore it and get to the Hall. Okay?"

"Ok." She agreed.

"I know this is weird timing, but when we get home and have time, I'd like to take you on a date. A real, planned out, just you and me date. What do you think? We'll have to make time for it. You and I both know that we will never have a chance if we don't make one."

The thought made her giddy.

"I love it. I can make time."

He smiled and bent his head down to kiss her. That's all he wanted. Time with her.

There was a quick knock at the door before it flew open and Bruce scurried into the room. His hair was sticking out in every direction. He closed the door behind him and locked the door. His pupils were large like an excited feline. Brynn chuckled at the similarities between Bruce and the cat she manifested that day. Things seemed so much easier back then.

She wouldn't go back though. She was the butt of everyone's joke back then. Never again.

"Are you both ready?" Bruce asked as he looked Brynn and Gideon over.

"Ish." Gideon replied in total honesty.

He was nervous about this mission. There was no talking Brynn out of it, though. He knew that. All he could do was hope to get them to the Hall in one piece and keep her safe.

Bruce cast an extra lock the bedroom door and started chanting. Soon, a bright portal swirling with different shades of yellow and gold appeared in front of the door. He was giving no consideration to Gideon's pre-trip hesitations.

"Remember, don't stray from the path. Don't be deceived. Get to the Hall and you will be in the clear."

"Got it. What kind of distractions will they try to use?" Brynn replied.

"Whatever kind will work. So be vigilant."

Gideon took her hand in his as they approached the portal. They stood before it and hesitated for a second. Brynn took a deep breath and then they took a step forward and disappeared from the bedroom.

When they arrived on the other side, it

hit hard like the last time they portaled somewhere. Things were hazy and off. The sky was blue with puffy cumulus clouds, but there was no visible sun. Birds flew high up in the air. The ground beneath them was covered in lush grass with a small dirt trail leading to the north.

Two things were missing that both of them noticed right away. Wind and scent. Something was definitely being concealed here. There were trees off in the distance, but they weren't moving. Things were still and quiet.

"Familiar and concerning." Gideon said as he looked around.

"Yeah." Brynn nodded as she tried to adjust. "I see why Bruce gave us that warning now. Things aren't what the seem here. It feels like the battle that day."

"Do you think casting something would help?"

"No. I think whatever glamour they have on this place is stronger than anything I have in my arsenal to counter it. I might not be able to cast here at all."

"Yeah, that makes sense. Let's get there then."

Thank God Bruce was able to give them some guidance on where to go once they got through the portal. He told them to travel north and they would eventually see their destination. With the sun being MIA, orientation was a little more difficult to get a handle on. Luckily, Gideon had a remarkable sense of direction.

"I was counting on the sun to navigate, but it seems like that won't be happening. Do you know where we are going?" Brynn asked as she squinted and searched the sky for that familiar bright spot.

"Yeah, I noticed that. Bruce said north which should be that way." He pointed to his right where there just so happened to be a path.

"How do you even know that?"

Gideon shrugged.

"I'm an animal, Brynn. I have a terrific sense of direction." He winked.

"Awesome. Hopefully, it doesn't take us long to get there."

Gideon grabbed Brynn's hand in his and they headed down the trail. Neither of them said anything about it, but they were both nervous. There was so much potentially riding on this. It needed to go well. They needed answers. Hopefully, the guidance they were seeking awaited them at the end of this trail.

SIXTEEN

Vincent closed his eyes and tried once again to summon Max, but he had no luck. He pulled out his phone and dialed Max's number. It went straight to voicemail. Desperate for resolution, he decided to send a text.

"Max, please. We need to talk."

Truth be told, it was killing him inside. He hated how Max was treating his daughters. In a weird way though, Max was his son. He felt very conflicted.

His phone rang and snapped him out of

his thoughts. Max.

"You can't avoid me forever, Max. We need to talk." He said once he answered the call.

"What's the point, Vince? Too much has happened. How do we get past this? I don't see how we can. That's why I blocked our connection. I don't want to hurt you too. This seemed easier."

"It doesn't have to be this way. It's not too late to apologize and everyone get on with life. It's not too far gone."

Max laughed.

"I love you man, but we both know it's too late for all of that."

Max was right and Vincent knew it. It *was* all too far gone.

"What about Fiona?"

"What about her?"

"Come on, Max. Don't play these bullshit games with me. I am your maker. She is my daughter. What the fuck do you think I am asking you?"

"I'm not gonna kill her. She's not a blood donor or anything like that. But I do intend to keep her with me."

Vincent sighed.

"You should know," Max continued "I intend to break our connection, not just block it."

Desperation flared inside of Vincent, but he couldn't let it show.

"Please reconsider that. At the very least, give it more time and thought. It won't be easy for either of us. It can be more of a detriment than people might be letting on."

"Perhaps." He hesitated. "Vincent?"

"Yeah?"

Max was quiet for a moment before letting out a sigh.

"Is she really his mate?"

"Yeah, man. Look, you know that stuff is predetermined. Don't hold it against her.

She didn't plan for it."

"It's hard not to, dude. It feels like she ripped my heart out and took a dump on it. It was all for nothing. Anyway, I guess I'll see ya around."

Max hung up.

"Damnit!" Vincent shouted as he slammed his phone down on the desk. He pounded his fist next to it.

Shyan poked her head in.

"Everything ok?" she asked.

"No. Come in. Close the door behind you please."

She came in and sat down across from him. He rubbed his face and leaned back in his chair.

"I talked to Max."

"How did it go?"

"Not as I hoped it would. He says he is going to break our bond."

Shyan cringed.

"That's going to be rough on you."

"I know. Now is not the time to be dealing with his. I asked him to give it some thought first. Hopefully, he does. I told him it would be tough for both of us."

Shyan walked around the desk to him and rubbed his shoulders. He closed his eyes and leaned his head back.

"Where are Brynn and Gideon?" he asked as he enjoyed the massage.

Shyan hesitated. She knew he wasn't going to like her answer.

"They are on their way to the Hall of Records." She could have lied about it, but that would only make it worse.

"What? By themselves?" In an instant, the rage returned.

"Calm down, Vinny. They will be fine. Bruce portaled them there. They know not to get distracted."

"They are young, Shyan. Young people

are impulsive. You remember what we were like. The chances we took. The utterly dumb things we did along the way. Brynn can be a bleeding heart."

"Brynn is too determined to fail. Plus, Gideon will keep her safe."

"Are you sure about that? He took her to the woods last night and Max attacked her. He was supposed to be keeping her safe then."

"Oh Vincent. Don't be like that. You know something else was going on last night. We shouldn't hold that against him."

"Something is still going on, Shyan. What has been set in motion isn't over. I can feel it."

"Have a little faith in them."

Vincent nodded before standing up. He wouldn't admit it, but he knew she was right. He stretched his arms wide and yawned.

"I need to head out for a bit. Raef caught the shifters responsible for the attack last night. I need to pay them a visit."

"I will let you know when Brynn and Gideon are back."

"Love you." He said before kissing her head.

"Love you more." She replied.

In the blink of an eye, he was gone.

•   •   •

Raef jumped when Vincent appeared next to him.

"Damn dude. I'll never get used to that vampire stuff." He laughed.

"Thanks for dealing with this so quickly." Vincent started. "Are they in there?"

He motioned to the door behind Raef. Vincent sent him the address to this safe house this morning. This was an ideal location for a safe house. It was isolated with thick concrete walls making it decently soundproof. The room behind Raef was a cell of sorts. A perfect interrogation room.

"Yeah. They're in there chained up. You know these guys have nothing to do with us, right? We're all animals, but not all of us are monsters."

"Yeah man, I know. You gonna be around when I'm done here?"

"I'll stick around for a bit."

Vincent nodded and sped into the room. The shifter prisoners both shrunk against the wall.

"It sounds like you boys had quite a night last night."

Neither shifter said anything.

"What's wrong?" Vincent unsheathed his fangs. "Cat got your tongue?"

"Please, sir. What are you going to do with us?" The man cowered on the floor.

"That all depends on your words over the next few minutes."

Both men sat up straight, giving

Vincent their full attention.

"You pathetic slugs killed four vampires last night. Sure, you probably think you killed four evil, blood thirsty monsters. Nope. You killed two mothers and two fathers. Four people who had NEVER taken the life of another. So, tell me about the motivation behind your behavior."

"W-w-we." One of them stuttered, "We were told to go there."

"Told by who?" Vincent stepped hard on the man's shin and broke his leg. He screamed out in pain.

"A shadow person. Fuck! I don't know dude. I couldn't make out a face. It was just a shadow! You broke Carl's leg!" he tried to comfort his friend.

"That must make you Dwayne. So tell me, Dwayne. What did this shadow promise you? Surely there was something important on the line to make you murder four innocent people?" He punched Dwayne in the face. His front tooth flew across the room. Blood splattered on Vincent.

"It said all we gotta do was kill a few vamps. If we made it out, it would give us the one thing we wanted the most." Carl spoke up.

"Which is what? What did you ask for, Dwayne? A bigger dick?" Sweat dropped down Vincent's temple.

"I didn't. It said it already knew what we wanted."

"How do you know it wasn't just a trick?"

"Because it promised to bring my son back, No one knows about my son. I'm from a different clan. He was gone before I came here. I've never brought him up since I've been here. No one could've known."

Vincent's mind raced. Could any of this *actually* be true?

"There has to be something you can tell me about this shadow person. Are you supposed to meet somewhere? How are they supposed to pay up?"

"No. I don't know, man. It was a

shadow. A SHADOW. The voice wasn't like a man or a woman. It was kind of in the middle. And it stunk like eggs."

That was it.

Vincent snapped Carl's neck before turning to Dwayne and dispatching him. He walked out of the room and started looking for Raef. That hole had something to do with all of this, but what? He needed to find out. Raef was sitting near the front door waiting on Vincent to finish up when he walked out of the room.

"You good?" Raef asked when he saw a bloody Vincent.

"Yeah. None of it's mine." He shrugged his shoulders.

"I figured. I'll take care of the cleanup."

"Thanks. I appreciate you finding them for me."

"Not a prob, dude." Raef sighed. "I think you're gonna have to pay it forward pretty fast, though. I talked to Daveson this morning. One of the packs was attacked by vampires last night."

"Fuck."

"Tell me about it, dude. I don't know what last night was all about, but it just keeps getting worse and worse. The more I hear about, the more I want to forget."

"Do me a favor. Keep an eye on that hole. It has a role to play in all of this. I just don't know quite what."

"I got you. I'll give you a call if anything comes up."

Thanks." Vincent remarked before disappearing just as quickly as he appeared.

Once he got home, he went straight to his office. He didn't check in with Shyan. Normally he would, but he needed to get right to business. He pulled out his phone and called Daveson.

"I appreciate the call, Vincent." Daveson said when he answered.

"What happened? Raef told me vampires attacked a pack, but that's all I know. Catch me up." Vincent had a pen and paper ready to take notes. He didn't want to forget anything.

"Right after the stars starting falling last night, two vampires showed up at a pack house. They killed five men. No one else was there at the time on account of the celestial event. From what I saw on the cameras, they walked in the house, killed my men, and left."

"Can you see them clearly on the cameras?"

"Crystal. I'm sending you their pictures now."

"How do you want this handled? Do you want them or shall I dispatch of them?"

"I'd like to make those bastards suffer for what they did. The pack deserves it. Just say the word and we will help retrieve them however we can."

"I'll be in touch. And Daveson, please don't think that these low lives represent the rest of us."

"No worries, man. Wolves attacked Raef

and Gideon last night. They don't represent me either. I'll talk to ya soon Vince."

He sighed when the call ended. His phone chirped as the photos from Daveson began to roll in. They really were crystal clear. He looked closely at the two vampires. He was relieved that Max wasn't one of them. Angelica and Flaethien. Not surprising. Two of the nastiest women he had come across. They would be easy to catch up with, at least.

Most people were creatures of habit and this was no exception. These girls had a habit. Most mystica avoided humans as much as they could. Humans were intrusive and they had too many questions. Angelica and Flaethien didn't care though. Not when they needed a fix. Their dealer hung out behind one of the dive bars in town. It would be the perfect place to catch them.

He sent the address to Daveson along with a note saying to check it out around 8 in the evenings. He would be there too, of course. Not just to lend a helping hand, but to show some solidarity.

He looked down at himself and realized

he was still covered in blood. Nothing like getting right down to business. He rubbed the side of his face with his fingers and felt the dried blood. He scurried from his office to his bedroom as quickly as he could, trying to avoid anyone seeing him in the state that he was in. Shyan was sitting at the dresser when he walked in. She gasped when she saw him.

"Don't worry. It's not my blood." He said before she asked any questions.

"I know that is supposed to make me feel relieved. Unfortunately, it just raises more questions."

"I caught up with the shits that attacked the coven house last night. They won't be hurting anyone else. I got right to business when I got home and completely forgot about my appearance."

"How long have you been home?"

"Just long enough to make a phone call. It appears a couple of vampires killed some wolves last night. I have been trying to coordinate their capture with Daveson."

Shyan walked over to Vincent and

began to unbutton his shirt. He lifted an eyebrow and grinned at her.

"Let me help you." she said softly.

Vincent couldn't help but wonder if his bloody, disheveled appearance was a turn on for his wife. She liked when he was a tough guy. No wonder his daughters kept his nerves in a snow globe.

SEVENTEEN

"How long do you think we have been walking down this trail?" Brynn asked Gideon as she wiped the sweat from her brow. She was clearly getting tired already.

"I'd say pretty close to an hour." Gideon responded, not even slightly out of breath.

A rustling in the trees brought them to a halt. Before either of them could say a word, a small wolf limped out of the tree line.

"Should we help it?" Brynn asked with sympathy in her voice.

"It's probably a trick." Gideon responded a bit coldly. "Let's keep going, but keep your eyes peeled."

Brynn nodded and they continued down the dusty path. As they passed the injured pup, it began to howl. Her heart broke.

"If all of the tricks are like this, it's gonna be tough. What if someone really does need help?"

"That's just a chance we will have to take. We have to be selfish right now. I know it's not the most noble feeling, but it's about survival. Everyone's life back at home might depend on it."

She knew that he was right. It didn't make it any easier, though. They kept walking forward. The small trail that they were walking along was dry and dusty. It didn't appear to be traveled much. The tree line on either side of the path began to get closer and closer.

"The trees are different here." Brynn remarked as she scanned the treetops and looked around. She was used to pine trees, oaks, magnolias. These were similar, but so slightly off. There was a blue tinge to the leaves. The trunks and branches were more green than brown.

"Yeah, I noticed that too. Have you looked at the clouds?"

Brynn looked up and took note of the wispy, cream-colored clouds above her. A horn sounded faintly in the distance.

"They must know we are here." She said as she stood on her tiptoes and strained her eyes trying to look ahead. "I think I might see something."

Gideon picked her up and put her on his shoulders.

"How's the view now?" he asked.

"I can definitely see the hall. It's still too far away to see much else." She held her hand over her eyes.

She hopped down and used her newfound flying abilities to float back down gracefully.

"Well, at least our target is in sight."

"HELP!" a voice shrieked from within the trees.

Brynn readied herself to run into the woods, but Gideon grabbed her shoulder and held her back.

"It's another trick, Brynn. We can't fall for it."

"What harm could it do just to venture in and look? Just double check, ya know?"

"It could do *a lot* of harm. Who's to say that we don't go look and get trapped in there?"

"I think you have a pretty good sense of direction. Surely we wouldn't get lost."

He appreciated how confident she was in his abilities. She was missing the point, though. They didn't know the extent of the trickery Bruce warned them about.

"Bruce warned us for a reason, darlin'. Please just trust me here. We have to keep going."

The voice in the woods began to wail. It went against all of Brynn's instincts to keep moving, but she did anyway. Gideon was right. The lives of everyone at home depended on this. It still sucked though.

"I'll be happy when we make it there." She sighed.

"Well, I suppose we could always expedite this. I can shift and you can either ride me or fly next to me."

"It *would* be a clever way to circumvent some of these distractions. I think I'll take a ride if you don't mind. Seems like it would be harder to get separated that way."

He handed her his clothes and she stuffed them in her backpack. Once he shifted, she climbed on his back and he took off toward the Hall. Brynn was right. It did help them avoid the distractions.

She held on tight as Gideon barreled down the path. Brynn decided to cast a shield around them and was surprised when it worked.

"I guess I *can* cast here." She said mostly to herself.

She thought about blasting them with every spell she knew, but she stopped herself.

Neither of them knew who they were going to encounter once they were at the Hall. She didn't want to risk overcasting and seeming inauthentic. This could be the only chance they got.

As they got close, Gideon slowed his pace. Once Brynn hopped off of his back, he shifted back into a human. She pulled his clothes out of her bag and handed them to him, making sure to eyeball him one good time first.

"I figured I'd get dressed before we get there in case we meet someone important. Hard to make a good impression with your wiener out." Gideon joked, making Brynn laugh.

"It would make a pretty big impression." She smiled and shrugged her shoulders. She could have sworn she saw him blush.

A gentle buzz in the distance began getting closer to them. Brynn braced for bees or some sort of pestilence but was surprised to see a group of hummingbirds fluttering around them.

"Hummingbirds?" Gideon said curiously.

"Yeah!" Brynn was excited. "It's a good sign. Hummingbirds are good luck. They represent love and devotion and are fierce defenders of their territory."

"I had no idea their wings could make so much noise." He chuckled as he buckled his belt. "How do I look?"

"Very presentable." She blew out a slow breath and rubbed her hand on her legs. She was nervous and it showed. "We can probably make it to the front door in about two minutes."

They both looked toward the tall white building ahead of them. The bright blue roof shimmered even without a sun in the sky. The architecture felt whimsical, Something more out of a dream than anything.

"I think two minutes is about right. You ready?"

Brynn said nothing, just grabbed Gideon's hand, nodded, and started walking. Nearly two minutes later, they were at the front door. She was relieved that there were no last-minute distractions or derailments.

She raised her hand to knock when the door opened. A small old man wearing a crisp blue suit stood before them. It was almost the same shade as the roof.

"Welcome Brynn and Gideon." He stepped to the side and gestured with his hand. "Please come in. We have been expecting you. My name is Gabriel. I will be your guide today."

"Nice to meet you, Gabriel. Thank you for allowing us to be here."

Brynn and Gideon cautiously walked into the hall. Gabriel closed the door and locked it before turning around.

"Do not worry about the door lock. You are free to leave at any time. We don't let just anyone in here. Thus, the locked door. Please follow me. I do not hold the answers that you seek. However, I will escort you to the one who does."

They followed quietly behind Gabriel, still not saying much. He led them down a long corridor. The heels of Brynn's shoes clicked loudly on the marble floor, leaving an echo trailing behind. It was beautiful. Bright white with veins of gold running throughout. The interior was bright and extremely detailed. She felt like a pauper in a palace.

When they got to a set of ornate mahogany double doors, Gabriel paused.

"What you seek is beyond here. Enter when you are ready and only then."

He bowed his head before walking away.

"You ready?" Gideon asked Brynn with his hand on the doorknob.

"As ready as I'm gonna be."

Gideon opened the door and they were instantly blinded by light. They squinted their eyes hard and continued moving forward. Once the door shut behind them, the room dimmed enough to relax their vision. A tall figure with large angel wings came into view. Brynn gasped.

"An angel." She said quietly, barely

loud enough for Gideon to hear.

"Yes, Brynn. I am an angel. My name is Aeriethrael. Please sit down. I have come to give you information and answers what questions I am able."

Aeriethrael was a tall, slender looking woman. Her golden blonde curls fell all around her face, framing it perfectly. Her bright red lips curled into a smile. As Brynn studied her full set of feathery wings, she felt awe struck. The angel motioned toward the two brown leather couches in the center of the room. Brynn and Gideon walked to them and sat down next to each other. Aeriethrael sat down across from them.

"Tell me. Why have the two of you come here?" the angel asked.

"To get answers so that we can help our people and keep them safe." Brynn responded. "But you already knew that, didn't you?"

"Yes. I do know the answers that you seek. However, you must ask them yourself to get the guidance. I am... limited."

Brynn had been thinking about the

questions she had since Bruce first mentioned the Hall of Records. Now that the time had come to voice them, words evaded her. This was so important. She rubbed her sweaty palms on her pants. Gideon placed his hand on her knee. His calm energy radiated onto her. She exhaled slowly.

"Why me?" She asked softly, almost as if she were afraid to say the words out loud.

"To put it simply... it is your destiny. Your lineage is sacred. Chosen by God himself to keep the balance and peace. Just as the stars have a job ordained by God to carry out, so do you. The turmoil has been building for many generations. You shall see the people through the pinnacle of turbulence."

"What if I can't do it?"

"But you can. Why do you think Gideon is your mate? Have you ever heard of such a pairing? Even the stars thought it was crazy when they were handed the order. They said it had to be a mistake, but God simply laughed. He knew what he was doing and he does not make mistakes. Together, you will see this through."

"Our tattoos." Gideon said almost as if he had unintentionally said a thought out loud.

"A gift. With time, you will learn to understand them and their purpose. Pay attention. There is a reason for each of them. No other two people have ever had such a gift and no two shall ever have it again."

The magnitude of that statement hung in Brynn's mind. The implications of it a bit overwhelming.

"What will be the outcome of all of this?"

Aeriethrael was silent for a moment. She looked toward the fireplace a bit solemnly.

"There are too many variables to tell you right now. Yes there is a path and a destiny. Much like this place, however, there will be distractions and tricks along the way. If you do not let them deter you, victory will be sweet. If you give in to them, the future gets progressively dimmer."

Brynn and Gideon nodded. Their minds were struggling against the weight of what they were being told.

"Are you able to tell us what to do next?" Brynn was desperate for something.

"Only that you should focus on your current mission... building relationships. You will need allies in the coming days."

"What is that hole?" Gideon asked grimly.

Aericthrael looked at him with a hard to explain intensity.

"To put it simply, that hole is evil. Please understand that demons walk amongst you just as angels do. There are dark forces that want you to fail. When you return, tell your father that hole is *exactly* what he thinks it is. That is all he will need to know.

I hate to be brief, but the two of you need to be returning soon."

Brynn's stomach turned. This was sounding worse and worse.

"Is there any advice you can give us before we go?"

"You have eyes to see and ears to hear. Utilize them. The people you love might not be trustworthy. Those you dislike might be more noble than you think. Do not give someone a pass simply because they are important to you. People can always be betrayed.

Treat each other well. You are perfect for each other in every way. The yin to the other's yang. Together, you are an unstoppable force. Never have there ever been two people so perfectly tailor made for each other. Utilize it.

Remember who you are, Brynn. Wear those wings proudly. You are chosen. All those years of struggle for you were critical for your development. It made you resilient. Strong. Persecuted because you were different. Now that difference will have people bowing to you.

Now, you must be getting back. When you open those doors, you will walk into the room from which you left to journey here."

"Will we see you again?" Brynn asked before getting up.

"Hopefully not for a long time. Now,

along you go." Aeriethrael stood up and motioned toward the door.

They did as she requested and walked to the door.

"By the way, here's a little gift." Aeriethrael snapped her fingers and Brynn heard a low buzz in her ears. It only lasted for a moment before disappearing. "When you get back, it should be a little easier to tap into your angel powers."

"Thank you." Brynn said quietly, unsure of what that meant. She grabbed Gideon's hand.

He opened the door and the bright light hit them harshly in the face. They both squinted their eyes before walking through the doorway. In an instant, they were back in their bedroom.

EIGHTEEN

Bruce let out a big sigh of relief as soon as Brynn and Gideon reappeared in the bedroom. Had he been holding his breath the entire time they were gone?

"Thank the heavens that you have made it back." He sounded too relieved.

"Did you think we wouldn't?" Gideon raised an eyebrow.

Bruce paused for a moment and his cat-like pupils dilated. His nose twitched as he rubbed his mustache.

"Perhaps the mission was a bit more dangerous than I let on originally."

"It wasn't too bad." Brynn shrugged.

"Gideon did a good job keeping me focused."

"And I shifted and we just ran for most of it." Gideon contributed.

"Smart. Don't give the distractions time to distract." Bruce replied simply.

"Did you already know what would be waiting for us at the Hall of Records?" Brynn asked.

She rubbed her ears. She kept hearing low static. Maybe it was going to take her a few minutes to readjust to being back on this plane. Even if it had been difficult the last time she portaled, her adrenaline would have been too high to even notice.

"No. I did not know anything about what your journey would entail. I just knew that you needed to go, my lady."

"Thank you, Bruce."

Bruce closed the portal, unlocked the door, and Brynn eagerly headed out of the room. She had to tell her dad what the angel told her about the hole right away. What did he know?

She found him sitting in his office. He looked like he had seen better days. The skin under his eyes was dark. His hair was disheveled.

"What the hell were you thinking going somewhere so dangerous?" Vincent boomed as soon as she walked into the room.

Brynn was caught off guard. She shouldn't have been though. Of course he wouldn't be happy about her taking off like that without a word. Especially since it was more dangerous than she thought. Gideon lingered outside of the door for a moment.

"You'd better get your ass in here too. And close the door behind you."

Gideon walked in quickly and did as he was told.

"Both of you sit down. I'll ask again. What the hell were you thinking? Do you know how easily you could have been killed? Or trapped in an optical illusion until it was too late to escape that place? Let me ask you this. How much research did *either* of you even put into this place before you hopped right through a portal?"

They both hesitated. They didn't know which question to address first.

"You're right. We didn't do the research. I know you're pissed and I get it. The truth is, we trusted our gut and everything was fine. I kept her safe. Chew us out as much as you want. You're her father and you have that right and obligation. I get it. But once you can get past it, you are going to hear what Brynn has to tell you."

Vincent pressed his lips together for a moment. He was furious that they so carelessly went there. He was even more angry that Gideon was right. They were safe. By the looks of it, they didn't even have a single scratch on them. He sat back in his chair.

"Go ahead, Brynn. I'm listening." He wasn't letting Gideon do all of the talking for her.

"Well, I will spare you the details on getting to the Hall other than to tell you that you would have been proud of Gideon. Once we were there, we met with an angel. Her name is Aeriethrael. Gideon asked her about the hole and she said that it is evil. She also said to tell you that it is exactly what you think it is.”

Vincent was speechless. Not only was Brynn so blessed that she met an angel, but that same angel had a message for *him*. A confirmation at that.

“Dad?”

Vincent looked up at Brynn quickly. He was lost in thought when he heard her voice. It suddenly felt like the weight of the world was on his shoulders.

“What is that hole?”

The angel was right. It is evil. Well, worse than that really. It is where evil spawned.”

“What? Like it’s a hole to hell or something?”

“Something like that. I’m sure it is the source of the attacks. I know it appeared after everything started. But they are definitely connected.”

“What do we do about it?” Gideon

finally spoke up.

"I'm not sure, but I know someone who might. I need to go see an old friend. Brynn, please tell your mother I will be back soon. And no more field trips!"

"Where are you going?"

"I'm afraid that I can't say. I promise I will tell you everything when I get back."

Brynn nodded and Vincent was gone in a flash.

"That could have gone worse." Gideon joked.

Brynn laughed as she blew out a sigh of relief and elbowed him in the side. Her phone buzzed.

Fiona.

She opened the text message and rolled her eyes. It was a picture of Fiona half-naked, wearing a bright pink bra. She was lounging on Max's chest. They were both smiling.

"She looks like a whore." Gideon said causally as he looked over her shoulder.

Her hair was dyed black. Her makeup thick. Bright red lipstick was caked on her lips.

"I'm sick of this stupid stuff." Brynn sighed, feeling a little defeated.

"My patience is wearing thin to be perfectly honest. I'm over this manipulative fuck boy bullshit." He said as he stood up and extended his hand to Brynn.

She took his hand and they started walking toward the door. Brynn rubbed her ears again. The static was still there. It seemed to be getting worse. She could've sworn that she had heard a faint voice or two.

"What's up with you?" Gideon asked as they made their way down the hall.

"I don't know. It's my ears. It sounds like static. Almost like a radio station that can't quite come in. I could have sworn I heard a couple of voices earlier."

"When did it start?"

"Well, I initially thought it started when we got back. That's not right, though. It started when the angel snapped.”

“When she said it would be easier to tap into your angel powers?”

“Yeah, actually.”

“Close your eyes and focus on it. Can you hear any voices?”

Brynn did as Gideon suggested and closed her eyes. She focused on the sound of the static. Once she listened for a moment, it began to sound more like a low frequency. Eventually, there were whispers. She tried to fixate on what we being said.

“Brynn.” She heard in a low tone.

“Yes?” She tried to answer mentally, feeling like an absolute weirdo.

“The fate of the fae is in your hands. You could not achieve greatness before, because you were intertwined with evil. Max is your enemy. Now that you are with your chosen mate, the one in the world who is most like you, you have a chance to prevail.”

“Who are you?” Brynn asked.

"My name is Ezeriel."

"Are you an angel?"

"Yes."

Brynn's stomach turned into a knot. That's what Aeriethrael did for her. She was tapped into some sort of angel frequency now. She opened her eyes and looked at Gideon.

"Angel radio?" he asked with a half grin.

"Something like that." She nodded. "Where are we going, anyway?" she asked once they started walking again.

"We need to go see the wolves. Daveson sounded bad when I spoke to him earlier. I think a visit to solidify our alliance would be a good idea."

Brynn agreed and followed Gideon to the truck. She continued trying to focus on the frequency in her head. There had to be a way to control it somehow.

"I wish I could either figure out how to use this or turn it off. So far, it's just a headache.”

“You’re smart. You will figure it out. Surely you will be able to turn it up or down... kinda like the radio. You’ll have to hone your skills.”

“Yeah, that’s what I thought too.” She rubbed her temple.

She was shocked to look out the truck window and see that they were almost to the pack house already.

“We got here fast.” She said to Gideon. He chuckled.

“Not really. You have just been in deep thought over there. You didn’t even hear me singing, did you?”

She shot him a skeptical look.

“You were singing?”

“No, not really.” He laughed. “I don’t think you’re ready for this beautiful singing voice of mine.”

“Is that so?”

"Absolutely! You won't be able to keep your hands off of me once you hear it." He winked.

Brynn laughed and Gideon pulled down Daveson's driveway.

It was long and lined with pine trees. It was decently concealed from the road and the surrounding woods made it feel very private. Once the driveway ended, it opened up to a vast compound. Sitting high on a hill in the distance was a large, nice house.

"That must be the pack house." Brynn said when she spotted it.

"Yes ma'am. I forgot you've never been out here. Some of these wolves can be pretty tough, so just keep a keen eye on them. Don't worry, you won't be out of my sight."

"I'm not worried." She replied simply.

When they pulled up to the pack house, Daveson was standing on the front porch. He raised his hand in the air as they parked the truck.

"Welcome to wolf land, Queenie."

Daveson quipped when Brynn got out of the truck.

"Thanks for having me." She replied, eyeballing the other wolves standing around Daveson.

She and Gideon walked up to the porch to greet everyone. One by one, Daveson introduced them. When he got to the grimy looking fellow in the middle, the hair on Brynn's arms stood up.

"Beware." She heard softly in a celestial type of voice.

The guy gave her the creeps. His dark hair was long and stringy. Something about his grin felt grimy... like the smile of a swindler. He had faded tattoos that were difficult to make out against his skin. They might have been easier to see if it were black ink, but the faded blue-green color blurred against his copper skin.

Gideon felt his tattoo tingle and he was suddenly on high alert. He didn't know what was up with this guy, but there was definitely something there.

"Now that you've met the pack, come inside and we can talk."

They followed Daveson inside of the house. It looked pretty similar to what Brynn expected. Lots of wood. Wood floors... wood walls... wood ceiling. It was dark and somehow cozy.

"Babe!" Daveson shouted. "We have company."

A blonde woman with a small frame appeared in an instant.

"This is Adrienne, my Luna. Adrienne, this is Gideon and Brynn."

"Brynn? You're the new fairy queen, aren't you?"

"That's me." Brynn blushed. She might never get used to the attention or notoriety this new world brought her way.

"Let's sit down in the living room." Daveson said as he led them through the house.

The living room was admittedly pretty

impressive. The vaulted ceilings were trumped only by the wall of windows. Bright white frames accentuated the floor to ceiling glass. It overlooked the backside of the hill that the house was sitting on. Across the land you could see rolling hills covered in lush green grass and a multitude of free-range animals. A small creek ran through the center from one tree line to the other.

"I am so sorry to hear about the loss your pack has experienced." Brynn said as they sat down.

"Thank you. I don't know what happened during that damn star show, but it made people hysterical."

"I know, man. This just don't make sense." Gideon shook his head.

"Luckily, Vincent is a man of his word and the vampires in question will be dispatched soon."

"I hope you know that my father would never condone such an atrocity. This alliance is very important to us." Brynn explained.

"Likewise. Just as the wolves that

attacked Gideon and Raef were not acting on my behalf, the same can be said for the rest of the attacks."

"Is there anything we can do to help you guys?" She asked.

"I don't want to lose any more pack members. What do you two think about everyone doing some training together? It would give everyone a chance to be a little prepared in the future."

"I think that's a great idea. Training with Gideon before the battle really helped me learn about my abilities. I'll call a meeting in the next week so we can all discuss it and implement some plans."

"Thank you. I look forward to it. Let me know if the pack can do anything for you in the meantime.

Brynn nodded and they all stood up. Daveson escorted them back to the truck. As she walked past Jeremy, the creep from earlier, he nodded at her and smiled. She shivered. They exchanged pleasantries with Daveson and Adrienne and headed home.

"Have you ever met that guy before?" Brynn asked once they were back on the main road.

"Jeremy? No, I haven't."

"You immediately knew who I was talking about. Did you get bad vibes from him too?"

"My tattoo tingled. It was either him or you thinking something about him. I don't really know which. Did you feel it in your tattoo?"

"No. I heard a voice say "beware" in my head. Like a small, celestial voice."

"Well, I hope you tell the angels thanks for the heads up." He chuckled.

"Yeah, I assume that's what that was. I gotta figure out how to fine tune this."

They pulled back onto the compound as she continued to focus on the new commotion in her head.

NINETEEN

Brynn was relieved to see that Vincent was home when they arrived. She hoped that he had some answers. Shyan was hovering around the front door when they walked in.

"There you two are. Your father is back and he wants to have a family meeting. That includes you, of course, Gideon."

They didn't offer any explanation as to where they had been, they just followed Shyan to Vincent's office. He was sitting at his desk when they walked in. Shyan closed the door behind her and turned the lock. Once everyone got seated, she cast a silence bubble around them.

Brynn got a little nervous. This must be something pretty serious. They didn't do this with other conversations.

"Kids, I'm sorry I left so abruptly earlier." Vincent started.

"Where did you go?" Brynn asked, remembering his earlier promise of answers.

"I went to see a cousin. Like you and I, Brynn, he has angel wings. In fact, he was the one that showed up to get my father that night. His journey in life has shown him some pretty grim things. We are extremely fortunate to not have been to the places he has.

He used to mention a stairway to Hell when I was young. In fact, when the song Stairway to Heaven came out, he could barely shut up about it. When I saw that hole and smelled the sulfur, it was the first thing I thought about."

"So, you went to tell him about this hole."

"Yes. I needed any type of information

he had. I always thought it was babble. Either way, I needed anything I could get out of him. He lives about four hours north of here in the foothills. The secluded location gave us nothing but peace and opportunity to talk. I tried to convince him to come back with me, but I was unsuccessful."

"Why wouldn't he come?"

"Think of him as one of the soldiers you learned about in school. They go to war, see some gruesome things, and when they come back... well, as you can image, some of them have a hard time readjusting to everyday life. It just is what it is. Mack is a lot like that."

"What did you find out from him?" She asked with both hope and worry in her voice.

"Everything. I think he was right this entire time. All the years I wrote it off... he was right all along."

"Can we close the hole? How do we get rid of it?" Gideon spoke up.

"Yes, it can be closed and banished. To do that, you have to find the person responsible for it being there. They are the only one who can close it. Either by word or by death."

Brynn felt defeated. The task at hand sounded impossible.

"How do we do that?" She asked.

"There will be a signature. We have to cast the right reveal spell and we will see it."

"Do you know which spell is the right one?"

"No, but I know that we know enough of them to figure it out." His confidence made her smile.

"And what if we can't close it? What happens then?"

Vincent's demeanor turn downward, giving off hopeless vibes.

"Evil will keep coming out of that hole unless we stop it. And I don't just mean evil spirits or bad mojo. I mean actual demons that want to possess and influence people. We have been able to keep it at bay so far, but we can't forever. Either we get rid of it, or we prepare for a war that we didn't expect to fight in our lifetime. One that only God himself could win."

"Let's get this bad omen closed up and out of here then." Gideon said with enthusiasm.

"You guys ready for a family trip to the woods?"

Brynn and Gideon nodded.

"Good. Bruce and Madeleine are meeting us there."

"I packed snacks to bring with us." Shyan spoke up before dispelling the silencing bubble.

"Perfect." Gideon exclaimed. "My stomach hasn't stopped growling."

"That's what reminded me." Shyan giggled. "Let's swing through the kitchen on our way out."

The four of them hopped into Vincent's SUV after grabbing their snacks and heading outside. Everyone munched on the drive to the woods. Gideon's stomach growled the entire trip despite shoveling down a lot of deli meat and cheese. He kept telling Shyan that she should start a charcuterie business. He meant it. Her snacks were top of the line. And it was hard to satisfy a shifter's appetite. A bear at that.

Once they made it to their parking spot and into the tree line, Gideon shifted while the girls flew and Vincent used his vampire speed to get to the hole. As promised, Bruce and Madeleine were there waiting for them.

"Thanks for coming." Vincent said.

"I heard you needed an expert spell caster." Madeleine joked.

"Like I said on the phone, we need a certain reveal spell. Unfortunately, I don't know which one we need. We are looking for a signature of some sort. It could be an image, a scent, even an object of the person of interest."

"Well..." Bruce began to think. "I suppose we should start with the easiest and go from there."

Madeleine wasted no time before she began to cast. Shyan stepped in from time to time to give her sister a break, but the entire process was taking longer than any of them expected it to. She would periodically cast spells to recharge their magic and give them some extra focus.

Eventually, Madeleine found the right spell. Red sparks sprung from the hole like fireworks and everyone jumped back. An image started to form above the hole. It almost looked like a projection. It started blurry before slowly coming into focus. It was a face. A familiar one at that.

Max.

"This has gone TOO FAR!" Vincent boomed and the image of Max shattered into hundreds of pieces before dissolving into thin air. "Let's all get back to the house. We need to discuss a resolution. Bruce and Madeleine, that includes you."

Everyone agreed and made their way back to the fairy compound. Once there, they grabbed a few more snacks from the kitchen on their way to the study. Just as before,

Shyan cast a silencing bubble around them once they were all in the room.

"Max has to be stopped once and for all. I refuse to keep playing this game with him. There are bigger problems we need to be focusing on. I have tried to compel him, but he has me blocked. He has threatened to break our bond to each other."

Brynn gasped. She knew how detrimental that could be for her father. She heard that the pain something like that causes was almost as bad as it could get.

"I asked him to reconsider for a bit and so far it appears that he has. However, I think that time is extremely limited."

"We need to find a way to lure him somewhere." Gideon spoke up.

"Yes. That's smart. Once we have him, we can trap him. He can be dealt with easier if he is restrained." Bruce spoke up.

"That's all good and fine." Brynn began. "But how do we lure him at all? He clearly doesn't care about our opinion or what we have to say. He manipulates every situation.

Look at Fiona. She's pretty brainwashed at this point. I mean, she's sending me half naked pictures of herself to try to prove some childish point. Max is behind all of it."

Everyone thought about it for a moment. She made a good point. Vincent couldn't compel him. There was a roof over his head. He had Fiona with him. What could they even hope to offer him?

"I offer him a quick and straightforward way to break our bond. I have him meet me in the woods. Everyone can be hiding. We get enough silver to hold him down and he won't be able to fight us."

"That could work." Bruce remarked. "When shall we do this?"

"Why waste any time? Let's do it tonight. I'm ready to be done with this charade." Vincent replied.

"How do we convince him to close the hole?" Brynn was curious.

"Between the pain from the silver and the offer of independence, he can't resist."

Everyone looked around at each other and nodded their heads in agreement.

"Everyone has to be in position before I make the call to him. With his speed, he could scope it out quickly. That would leave him open to notice slight differences created after your arrival. Everyone needs to get there, find a spot, and then good concealment spells need to be cast."

"I can do the casting." Madeleine volunteered.

"Don't go easy on it. Beef everyone up with as much as you can. There is no such thing as too much. They need to be strong. They need to be silent. And most importantly, they need to be completely concealed. Scent and all. Take a few minutes to gather everything you will need. Call me when you are all in position and concealed. Then just wait for us to arrive."

Brynn's stomach was filled with butterflies. Another face off with Max. She worried that Gideon was going to hurt him this time. Max deserved it. Despite it all, it still hurt her in a weird way. She never thought that Max would end up being her enemy. She tried to suppress it all. Gideon didn't need that clouding his mind.

As everyone filed out of the room, they went their separate ways. Everyone grabbed supplies, weapons, and food. They all met back up outside in the driveway. They couldn't take a vehicle this time. Max would definitely know something was up if they drove. There would be no great way to conceal the vehicle. It could be out of sight, yes, but masking certain scents was tough. Engine oil was one of them.

The girls all planned to fly, Gideon shifted already, and Bruce was getting there via some sort of warlock magic they were all pretty curious about.

"Wait!" Madeleine exclaimed. "I need to hide everyone's scent now. This way there are no traces of us along the way."

She cast a spell and once it was done, she gave everyone the green light to begin their journey. Brynn laughed when Bruce shrunk down into a cat and hopped onto Gideon's back for a ride. She knew there was something more to the catlike appearance.

They made their way to the woods as a group. Once there, they assembled in the trees all around the hole. They tried their best to cover all angles. Madeleine cast all of the spells that she could think of. Bruce chanted a few things as well before Shyan pulled out her phone and called Vincent.

"We're ready." She said when he answered.

"See you soon, kitten." He said before hanging up.

Vincent was right. It didn't take long for Max to show up. He looked around the area carefully, making sure he wasn't walking into a trap. He walked over to the hole and looked down at it for a moment. He stared longingly at it before smiling and zipping away. Everyone was relieved when he left. Madeleine must have done a good job casting because he didn't seem skeptical at all.

Pretty soon, Vincent arrived. He sat down on a stump close to the hole while he waiting for Max to show back up. Everyone stood silently, waiting on pins and needles for the show to begin.

Max showed back up before long, but he brought one huge complication with him. Fiona. Vincent pulled out his phone and sent a text to Bruce.

"If she gets too close, cast something to restrain her. I don't care if you have to string her up in the air. Keep her out of the way."

Bruce read the message but didn't send one back. Vincent needed to focus.

"I'm here as promised." Max announced as he strode toward Vincent. "I even brought a guest. I thought you might like some visual proof that she is doing fine."

Vincent was surprised by Fiona's new image. Jet black hair, thick makeup, skanky clothing. He sighed. What had Max turned her into.

"Sweetheart." Vincent said.

Fiona said nothing back, offering only an exaggerated eye roll.

Might as well get this show on the road.

TWENTY

"NOW!" Vincent shouted as everyone sprung into action.

In an instant, Fiona flew up into the air and was suspended in a thick bubble, leaving her unable to move or fight. Bruce focused all of his energy keeping her safely there. She was angry. Thrashing around the bubble, banging on the side with her fists.

Gideon grabbed a thick silver chain by his feet and swung it around hard like a lasso. When he released it, it wrapped around Max's arms and upper body. He was instantly immobilized. This amount of silver was too much for him to fight against.

"What the fuck is this?" Max strained to yell. "Your idea of an intervention? I already told you dude, there is no going back at this point."

"You're right, son. There is no going back. You have gone too damn far this time. I know it was you that opened this portal." Vincent howled.

Max laughed maniacally.

"Why did you do it, son?"

Max shrugged and thought for a moment.

"To make the best weapon anyone has ever seen before." He motioned toward Fiona before smiling.

"You sick son of a bitch!" Vincent roared.

"Do whatever you want to me. You can't undo what is already done. But Vincent, don't forget... you made me into this monster. Deep down inside, you know that. Would we be here now if you had just left me alone? Take your time. I'll wait."

The concealment spells suddenly sputtered out and Max saw everyone around him. He laughed and spit at the ground. His eyes darkened as a wicked expression formed on his face.

"Well, well, well. It looks like the queen of the sluts is here too. This is quite the trap you have all created. Kind of pathetic, but that's to be expected with such a weak-minded leader. You should have seen how easy it was to get her trapped in that spell. Almost as easy as getting into her pants. I should have just killed her then. Hey, we all make mistakes I guess."

Gideon growled.

"Aww. What's wrong wittle bear cub? Embarrassed that you're stuck with the frigid sister? Looks like I won this one after all. It's too bad... when she gets bored with you, you won't be able to bang her little sister. She's mine. And let me tell you..." He licked his lips. "She tastes so sweet."

"Enough!" Vincent bellowed before

speeding toward Max.

Vincent pulled the sword on his side out of its sheath. With one swift movement, he swung the blade and made contact with Max's neck. No one saw it coming. His head flew through the air, rolling once it hit the ground, and coming to a rest a Brynn's feet. She stood in horror and what she just witnessed. The headless body slowly buckled and fell to the ground.

Gideon grabbed her arm and pulled her away and into his chest. He wasn't an idiot. She might have hated Max, but she loved him once. She didn't need to stand there staring at his severed head.

"NO!" Fiona screamed, bursting the bubble that she was suspended in.

Everyone looked up quickly. Fiona hit the ground hard, but popped back up like it was nothing. She started to run immediately. Before she had a chance to get to Max, Vincent bent down and set his head on fire. Brynn winced and buried her face into Gideon's chest.

"That's the only way to be sure that he

doesn't come back." Vincent stated plainly to no one in particular.

Fiona shrieked so loudly that everyone almost hit their knees. In an instant, jet black wings emerged from her back. They were huge and feathery, just like Brynn's. Everyone gasped. Black feathers began to fall all around them.

The smell of sulfur filled the air. When Fiona looked up at the crowd, she met everyone's stare with cold black eyes. The torment on her face was evident. She threw her head back and began to chant quickly before turning into a flock of ravens and flying away. The birds were loud until the sight of them disappeared.

The ground began to rumble by the hole and a thick cloud of black smoke shot into the sky quickly. Nearby birds screeched loudly in the night sky and with a loud boom, the hole imploded. Dust filled the air and everyone quickly shielded their eyes. When the dirt and dust all settled, the hole was gone and the ground was even. No evidence left behind. Just disturbed dirt and vegetation.

Everyone stood in stunned silence as they tried to process everything that had just happened. Max was dead and dismembered. Fiona had just turned into some sort of evil fairy angel. Everyone thought they would be able to convince Fiona to come home with them. Instead, Brynn had a sinking feeling that she had just become their new adversary.

Brynn's phone began to ring. She pulled it from her pocket and looked at the called id. It was Quyen.

"Hello?" She answered with a shaky voice before clearing her throat.

"Brynn? What happened? The ground was shaking and after it stopped, the prophecy... it's going crazy. A new passage has appeared and it looks pretty important. Are you okay?"

"We are all in the woods behind your house right now. We will be there soon."

She hung up the phone before Quyen responded and put it back in her pocket. Everyone was staring at her.

"That was Quyen. She said something

is going on with the prophecy. There's more of it now. We need to go to her house. It's on the other side of those magnolia trees." She pointed ahead of her toward the tree line.

No one bothered flying or shifting to get there. They all just solemnly started walking in that direction. Like zombies. Before he joined them, Vincent lit what was left of Max's body on fire. As he smoldered behind them, Brynn tried to focus on other things. She wasn't ready to accept the reality of what had just happened. Gideon kept his arm around her tightly. Her mate runes vibrated lightly.

"Goodbye, Maximillian." Brynn heard Vincent say quietly before joining the group.

Her heart broke for her father. A maker having to kill his own progeny. It wasn't supposed to be this way. How he was up and walking with them was beyond her. He had to be in agony.

Once they made it through the trees, they could see Quyen waiting on the front porch. She was surprised once she saw how shell shocked everyone seemed to be. She couldn't help but wonder what happened. She knew it had to have been bad.

"It looks like everyone has had a rough night. Come in, have some tea."

Everyone followed her inside the house. She grabbed the tea kettle and brought it in the living room where everyone had assembled. Gideon grabbed the teacups out of the cabinet for her. She assembled them around the table and started pouring.

"Tell us about the prophecy, Q." Brynn said as Quyen tried to work off her nervous energy.

"Whatever just happened to you all in the woods... well, there is more prophecy revealed now. Would you like me to read it to everyone or just you?"

"Go ahead and just read it to all of us. You have my permission. That will make it easier than me telling everyone by memory later."

She grabbed the book from the table and cleared her throat before reading.

"A divide is forged. A line in the sands eternally drawn. What is done cannot be undone.

A battle between good and evil shall decide the fates of all mystica.

Each side united. One led by the damned. The other by righteousness. Day will meet night. New friends slain by the darkness will meet old friends led astray.

Two souls unified. One broken heart. One focused soldier can trump a divided pair.

Good versus evil.

One angelic. One demonic.

Only one side can prevail."

Everyone looked at each other, but no one said a word.

"What happened out there guys?" Quyen asked before sitting down.

Brynn sighed and said a quick prayer that she wouldn't cry. She was trying hard to keep her emotions in check. She didn't want to look weak. She didn't want to make Gideon feel bad either. It was overwhelming.

"To make a long story short... Max is dead and Fiona just sprouted out jet black angel wings before turning into a flock of ravens and flying away to God knows where."

"Wow." Quyen said, trying to process what Brynn just told her. "That's some pretty heavy stuff. What happened to Max?"

"Dad killed him."

Quyen opened her mouth to respond, but she had nothing. She just closed her mouth and frowned.

"Yeah. Definitely not how any of us were expecting our night to end, I think." Brynn said, trying to sound lighthearted.

"So that prophecy is saying what, that Fiona is evil now?" Gideon asked.

"Max said he made the perfect weapon. It looks like he was right." Vincent was monotone despite his best effort to seem more optimistic. He wasn't fooling anyone.

"Vincent, you must be in pain. Could I offer you any type of tincture or treatment?"

"Thank you, but no. I will be fine. Feeling this pain is a necessary price to pay for taking his life."

Quyen nodded at him, trying to quickly think of how to change the subject.

"What now?" she asked to no one in particular.

"We need to have a meeting." Brynn sighed. "First thing tomorrow. I would say tonight if it wouldn't be too pushy."

"Yeah. Things have definitely escalated. Everyone should be on alert." Gideon agreed. "Q why don't you stay with us or Raef tonight? With all of the craziness, you probably shouldn't be alone."

She agreed and everyone finished their tea. Once Quyen was ready to go, everyone piled into her truck and they headed to Raef's house. Once they filled him in on the night's events and Quyen was settled in, everyone else headed back to the compound.

The ride was quiet and Vincent was thankful that Quyen let them borrow her truck for the night. Now that his adrenaline had subsided, his body was feeling the effects of losing Max. He was sweating and in pain. He couldn't use his vampire speed to get home now if he tried. Shyan sat next to him, slowly rubbing his back. He was thankful to have the little bit of comfort.

Once they were home, Bruce and Madeleine said their goodbyes at the door. They were eager to get home and rest. Everyone was too mentally exhausted for anything productive tonight anyway. Shyan helped Vincent into the house and got him right to bed. Rest was the only thing that would help him right now. Once he was settled, she snuck out to the garden to have some time away from the others.

She was trying to be strong for Vincent and Brynn, but her heart was broken. She knew after what she witnessed tonight, the Fiona she knew was gone forever. The spunky, confident little girl that she raised was no more. She was replaced by a dark force. That wasn't her daughter anymore. It was just a vessel for something evil.

She sat on the bench hugging her legs as she cried. This was her fault. If she hadn't turned her back on Vincent, if she had focused more on her family, if she hadn't lost sight of Fiona while Brynn was spellbound... things might be different now. It was like the prophecy said, though. What was done could not be undone.

Her baby girl was gone and that was a reality that she was going to have to find a way to cope with. She couldn't dwell on it. They were on the precipice of something far too important to get lost in grief right now. She could give herself this night to mourn, but she needed to be solid by daybreak.

Inside the house, things were quiet. Brynn felt broken inside. This was her fault. If she had just told Max to get lost... if she hadn't been his friend... he never would have spied on her. He never would have known that this world even existed. He would still be alive. That truth weighed heavily on her.

She sat on the ottoman at the foot of her bed motionless. Gideon turned the hot water knob on in the shower and let it get steamy. Once it was ready, he walked back to the bedroom.

"Come on. You'll feel better if you shower."

"I don't have the energy." She said softly.

"I know you don't. That's why I'm gonna do it for you."

Gideon extended his hand to her. She took it and he pulled her to her feet. They walked slowly to the bathroom.

"Lift your arms." Gideon said softly.

She lifted her hands over her head and he pulled off her shirt. He kissed the top of her head before taking the rest of her clothes off. He undressed as well before leading her into the shower. She stood under the hot water while he shampooed her hair. He took his time cleaning all of the dirt, blood, and bad memories off of her.

She closed her eyes and enjoyed the pampering. She appreciated Gideon. This wasn't anything sexual, just him being a good mate and knowing what she needed. Tears drifted down her face, quickly whisked away by the shower. He rinsed the conditioner out of her hair and turned the water off. He gently towel dried her before wrapping her in a white robe and picking her up. He carried her to the bed and laid her down before climbing in himself.

"Thank you." She said softly.

"No thanks needed pretty lady. I love you."

"I love you too."

He turned off the light and laid there in the dark, cradling her small frame. She closed her eyes and relaxed in the safety his arms provided.

TWENTY ONE

Gideon was calling people about the meeting before the sun came up. He didn't want Brynn to worry over it. She had enough on her plate. He knew that she was feeling conflicted. She hated Max. He was behind all of the bad things that happened to her recently. However, she used to love him. He was her first... everything. That would always occupy a small part of her heart. Of course it would hurt her to watch him die.

It didn't hurt his feelings. It wasn't personal. It was his job to make her life as easy as possible, though. That's what he was aiming to do.

He called Daveson first.

"Morning, Gid." He said with a voice that suggested Gideon woke him up.

"Sorry about the early phone call, Alpha, but some crazy shit went down last night. We need to have a meeting today. Can you make it?"

"Yeah, man. I'll be there. I'll bring my beta with me."

"Bring anyone you want to man. It's an all hands on deck kinda situation."

"Alright. What time?"

"Noon."

"See you then, bro."

He hung up and sent Quyen a text telling her what time the meeting was. He also asked her to bring her dad. He was a smart man. Seasoned, too. They could use his wisdom.

He called a few more people before

sneaking downstairs to grab some breakfast. He loaded up a tray full of eggs, sausage, bacon, pancakes, and a couple of bear claws. He loved that that was her favorite. He grabbed a cup of coffee and headed back to the bedroom. He was happy to see that she was still asleep when he waked back in. He placed everything on his nightstand before crawling back in bed.

"Good morning, beautiful." He whispered as he kissed her neck.

She snuggled up to him and smiled. He brushed the hair out of her face.

"I grabbed you some breakfast."

She opened one eye and surveyed the tray on his table before sitting up. It didn't take long for yesterday's memories to come flooding in. The heartache too.

"The meeting is set for noon." Gideon said as he placed the food on a tray for Brynn. He placed the cup of coffee next to her.

"Cream and two sugars." He said chipperly.

"Thank you." She said between bites.

"No thanks needed. You know I'm happy to do it." He snagged a few pieces of bacon from her plate.

"I know you are." She said with a smile.

After they finished their food and got dressed, Brynn headed to check on her dad. She knocked softly and her mom came to the door.

"How is he?" Brynn asked quietly.

Shyan stepped out of the room and closed the door quietly behind her. She looked awful. Her eyes were puffy and her skin was pale. She looked like she cried all night. Brynn didn't say anything, She knew why.

"He's ok. He just needs to rest. Bruce is on his way to doctor him up. In a couple of days he will be back in business."

"That's a good idea. Do you know if we need to get word to any vampires about the meeting?"

"I've already sent a few messages. You

can expect Gautier and Jacques. Dad's gonna have to sit this one out, I'm afraid."

Brynn nodded.

"Let us know if we can do anything." Gideon offered.

Shyan smiled and retreated back into her bedroom.

"Have you talked to Ecco?" Brynn asked as they made their way through the house.

"Yes. She will be here. That reminds me of a funny story I heard this morning. Guess who finally has a cell phone?"

"Who?"

"Raef."

"What made him have a change of heart?"

"Ecco. Apparently they went on a date. He got it to stay in touch with her."

Brynn laughed. She had heard it all now.

"We are going to need to have the meeting in a bigger space than usual." Brynn said as she led Gideon to a part of the house he hadn't ventured off into before.

"Just when I think I have been around this whole house, I discover something else."

Brynn opened a giant set of double doors. They creaked and groaned as if they had not been opened in some time. When they walked into the room, Gideon stared around in wonder. It was an enormous library with a meeting area in the middle.

"This should definitely do." He said as he continued to explore.

"We obviously don't use this very much. The court used to utilize this room for their bigger gatherings. I think tonight calls for it."

The two of them began to get the room ready for visitors. Brynn opened the curtains and dusted while Gideon got a good fire going. They didn't need the heat, just the ambiance. Brynn cast a quick spell once he was finished the keep the heat at bay. They were in the south, after all. It was always hot. Before long, Madeleine and Bruce appeared in the doorway.

"I had a feeling we would find you in here." Madeleine said as they walked into the room.

"I think we will have more people than usual. It made the most sense."

"I think it's perfect."

"Would you like us to usher your guests here once they arrive?" Bruce asked.

"That would be perfect, Bruce. Thank you. Have you checked in on my father yet?"

"Yes, my lady. I have. Don't you fret. He will be back on his feet in no time."

She nodded her head and continued to tidy up. She couldn't let herself dwell on what her dad had going on right now. She had too much on her plate. Bruce and Madeleine made their way to the front of the house. People would be arriving soon.

Raef, Quyen, and her father Gabe were the first to arrive.

"Uncle Gabe." Gideon said as he

extended his hand. "This is my mate, Brynn."

Gabe took Brynn's hand in his and kissed it.

"Pleasure to meet you."

He looked a lot like Gideon. It was easy to recognize that they were related. His hair was much shorter, but they had the same hazel eyes. Before they could exchange any more pleasantries, more people started arriving.

The wolves were next. Brynn shivered and she knew why before she even looked up. They brought him.

"Beware." She heard once again in her head.

"Don't worry. I know he's bad news." She tried to reply in her head.

"I hope it's okay that I brought my Luna." Daveson said as he approached Brynn.

"Of course. It's nice to see you again, Adrienne." Brynn smiled, avoiding eye contact with Jeremy.

She jumped when Gautier appeared in front of her. He chuckled when he noticed and Jacques elbowed him in the side.

"I told him not to do that." Jacques announced.

"It's fine. Good to see you, Gautier."

"Likewise, young lady. I am happy to step in while your father is... under the weather."

The vampires found a couple of chairs and sat down across from the wolves. One by one, more people began to file in the room. Some they expected to see, some they were surprised by. Raef perked up when Ecco walked in. She brought Rio again this time, but there was a new face with them as well.

"Brynn! Thank you for having us. This is Alec." She motioned to an olive-skinned man with dark hair. He had to have been an earth shifter. They sat down in the chairs next to Raef.

"Welcome, Alec." Brynn shook his hand before he found a seat.

Shyan was the last to arrive with a quick apology to Brynn for running late. Brynn waved off the unnecessary apology as her mom sat down next to Madeleine.

"Thank you all for coming on such short notice." Gideon announced, getting everyone's attention. "I knew this has been a rough week for everyone. Unfortunately, last night was the pinnacle for us. I will let Brynn explain."

"On the night of the... well, let's just call it the celestial event. We thought that a star crashed into the woods somewhere. Once we tracked it down, we found a hole. The area smelled of sulfur."

Soft murmurs began around the room.

"To make an exceedingly long story short, Gideon and I traveled to the Hall of Records. While there, we received a confirmation that the hole was exactly what we believed it to be... essentially a staircase to Hell."

"Why didn't you tell us about this?" Daveson asked in a disgruntled tone.

"Because we took care of it immediately."

"What do you mean you took care of it?" Ecco asked.

"We found out how to close the hole and we closed it." Her voice cracked slightly.

Brynn knew that she would have to go into more detail, but the truth of it all hurt so badly. She didn't want to say the words. Gideon would do it for her, but she felt like it was her responsibility. It was her fault and her burden to bear.

"Vincent found out how to close the hole. First, we had to find out who was behind it in the first place. Only they could close the hole, either by choice or by death."

She started to talk more and her voice hitched in her throat. Gideon put his hand on the back of her shoulder. She noticed most of the eyes in the room look at the gesture. The vibe in the room shifted. Everyone started to realize at once that Vincent wasn't in the room with them. They knew something was wrong. Brynn took a deep breath and focused.

"Believe in yourself." She heard in her head.

That celestial voice again. Only this time, she recognized it. It was Aeriethrael's voice. Brynn thought about the words and felt a twinge of courage in her chest.

"After casting numerous spells on the hole, we were able to find a signature left behind of the culprit. Max. We set a trap for him in the woods. Unfortunately, he was not willing to cooperate and he was dispatched. Upon his death, the hole imploded."

The room was silent. Everyone was in shock.

"That's why Vincent isn't joining us today. He is sick from the broken connection." Finn spoke up.

"Unfortunately, it's a little worse than that." Brynn sighed. "He is the one who killed Max. The intensity is more severe because of that. Luckily for us, Bruce is the best warlock around and he has done all he can to help. Vincent should be back on his feet very soon."

Brynn looked at Gideon, silently asking

him to handle the next part. It was more difficult to discuss. Luckily, he knew exactly what her expression meant.

"Last night's events with Max did lead to another problem that could impact every single one of us. It's why we called you here today. When he was asked why he created that hole, he insinuated that he used it to weaponize Brynn's sister Fiona. After he died, she transformed."

"Transformed?" Ecco was intrigued.

"Best I can describe it... she turned into a demon fairy." His southern accent made it sound even more ridiculous than it was. "In a fit of rage, she sprouted black feathery wings and chanted some crazy shit. Then she turned into a flock of ravens and flew away."

Each group started having quiet discussions amongst themselves. The room got loud quickly. This type of thing was unheard of. In any of their lifetimes, at least.

"Look, I wanted to have this meeting so we can formulate a plan. One plan for all of us. I don't know a lot about demonic possession and influence, but I am smart enough to know that this is dangerous territory. Have any of you dealt with something like this before?"

"I have." Jeremy spoke up.

Brynn almost rolled her eyes. Of course he had. Just one more confirmation that she was on the right track about him.

"A few years ago, I traveled out west to Oklahoma to help someone I knew as a pup. When I got out there, something was off about him. He wasn't the same guy I knew before. His eyes were darker than before and his personality was cold. Once I saw the amount of power he possessed, I knew it was evil. I have never met a more challenging opponent in my life."

"How did you deal with it?" Gideon asked.

"I went to the reservation looking for help. They had an old shaman that was relatively high-powered. Without their help, I don't think we could have defeated him."

"Did you have any allies fighting with you or was it all wolves?"

"Just us wolves. Having mixed ranks such as this group would have made it an easier fight. Either way, it is going to take some pretty strong magic."

"We need to decide today, as a group, what we want our future to be. For me, my goals are peace and unity. I want us all to be free and safe."

One by one everyone else in the room agreed.

"Then we need to get closer to each other and fast. I don't know what Fiona is planning. Part of me thinks she will just fade away and live her life, but the bigger part of me knows that she is evil now *and* she has a score to settle. We need to be prepared." Brynn announced.

"I still like the idea of training together. I say we start as quickly as we can. It will make us all stronger soldiers." Daveson spoke up.

"Does everyone else agree with group training?" She asked the room.

They all agreed. Even Gautier, which

surprised her. Vincent was so hesitant to call on him before, she kind of assumed that meant Gautier wasn't interested in any of this. Perhaps she was wrong.

"Fantastic. Does anyone have their heart set on training at a certain place? The way I see it, our options include each of our home bases. We have a lot of land here and all of you are more than welcomed to train here as often as you'd like. We can rotate as well."

"You have more space and resources here it seems. We would be open to primarily training here but rotating occasionally. Changing it up would probably keep us on our toes." Daveson suggested.

"I agree." Ecco started. "You have quite a bit of space here. Enough for all of us to spread out. I would be willing to host training occasionally as well. I have spoken with my people, and they are warming up to the idea of mingling with mystica society again."

Everyone began speaking back and forth, coming up with good idea about when and how to train. Brynn took a lot of notes as she listened to everyone's ideas. She was relieved that everyone was working together so well. She wished her father was there to see it. He would be proud.

TWENTY TWO

Hours of planning had passed and there was a knock at the door. Shyan opened the door to see a few fairies with carts of plates. Had they been in this meeting that long already? She stepped aside and let them in.

"We figured everyone could use a bite to eat. Let's take a minute to munch, but feel free to keep brainstorming in the meantime." Brynn announced.

Fairies laid out trays of different foods. They tried to have something to suit everyone. Lots of meat for the wolves, a few glasses of blood for the vampires, and the usual sandwiches and finger foods. Shyan and Madeleine grabbed the beverage pitchers and dismissed the other fairies.

"So, it sounds like everyone wants to start training tomorrow, which is great." Gideon said with a mouthful of steak sandwich. "Everyone that wants to train is welcome. If that means every member of your pack or group, so be it. The stronger we are, the better we are."

"If there are tools you want to bring, feel free. We can build obstacles if needed as well. This is a good opportunity to come together and be our absolute best."

"What about your sister?" Ecco asked. "Is there someone watching her? Do you need help gathering intel?"

"We could use some help. I know where she most likely is, but she would know I was coming from miles away."

"Understood. We can help with the recon. I'm sure she knows we elementals exist because of Max, but she won't be familiar with our scent."

"I think that's a fantastic idea. We also need everyone to keep their ears open and their eyes peeled. Someone had to have been helping Max. There is no way he would have known how to open up that hole. We need to find out who he was working with."

Ecco and her team nodded.

"I have another idea I'd like to discuss with everybody." Daveson stood up.

"By all means." Brynn responded, gesturing with her hand to indicate the floor was his.

"Being unified can make or break an army. A few soldiers can take down a whole platoon if they are united and the others aren't. I think we can all agree on that. Good leadership goes hand in hand with it. Optics also play into it. How do things look to that group of soldiers?

My point is, Brynn, you are in charge here. We have all accepted that. As Alpha, I can say admitting something like that isn't easy. The truth is what it is. You earned that spot, though. You led the battle against the court and freed so many of our people.

Allegiance is the best way any of us can express our gratitude.

I think that making it official would be great for optics. It would make us look united."

"What do you mean exactly?" Brynn asked apprehensively.

"Everyone calls you the Fairy Queen now, right? Well, I say we make you the Mystica Queen."

Brynn almost laughed out loud. She could understand the Fairy Queen thing. To be honest, she always took it more like a joke. She didn't think people were being serious when they said it. She freed prisoners, but wouldn't anyone in her shoes have done the same thing?

"Why would you want me to be your queen? I might call meetings and try to lead everyone, but I never expected anyone to do as I said. You're the Alpha. Why would you want to answer to someone? Especially a young woman? What's in it for you?" Brynn asked honestly.

"Because where I come from, you pay your debts and repay those who help you. My family members coming home changed the life of my pack in a way I couldn't have done myself. There is also the prophecy to think about."

One by one, every person in the room agreed with Daveson. Brynn felt her face get flushed. She wasn't prepared for this. She appreciated the sentiment, but the weight of it all seemed so heavy. When it got around to Quyen she looked at Brynn and smiled.

"I know this probably makes you feel overwhelmed Brynn, but they are right. I know the prophecy better than anyone. It's your destiny to be the leader of all of us, not just the fae."

"It's settled, then. We can have a ceremony of some sort to commemorate. Adrienne will plan it." Daveson decided.

Everyone clapped before Brynn could say anything in protest and she realized that she had no say in any of it. Quyen caught her eye and just smiled as if she were happy to see part of the prophecy come to pass.

"Alright then. I think we've made great progress today. I'll see everyone tomorrow morning for training." Gideon said as he pushed he chair back to stand up.

Brynn was thankful for the out. She looked up at him as he extended his hand to help her up. He winked and she smiled back at him.

"Thank you everyone for coming today." She said as people began to file out of the room.

Once everyone was gone, she blew out a long breath of air.

"Well, that was an interesting meeting." Brynn said, not quite knowing what to do with herself.

"One day you will see what the rest of us see." Gideon replied simply.

Brynn shrugged her shoulders.

"Wanna go outside and have a little one on one training? I knew we have a lot of it in our future, but a jump start is never a bad idea."

"You bet your cute little butt I do." He swatted her on the butt and they headed to their bedroom to change clothes.

Once they were outside, she was excited to train. She hadn't had a lot of time to train since being spellbound. She still felt rusty. That's why she seized her opportunity to pounce on Gideon before he was ready. Yeah, it was a lame move, but she needed to get the upper hand.

She jumped on his back and grabbed him, but he flung her off easily. She charged him again, this time sliding under him in an attempt to bring him down with her. He evaded her and jumped out of the way. He laughed before running toward her. He grabbed her and pinned her to the ground before she had a chance to act.

"I like this. It reminds me of the first time I got to be close to you. I knew that you were my mate then." He kissed her neck. "Do you know how hard it was to touch you and still control myself?" He kissed her again, making no attempt to move off of her.

She struggled beneath his weight, torn

between getting out from under him and surrendering herself to him. He kissed her again, rubbing his hand down her side to her waist. Her brain was hazy.

She thought about the day he was talking about. He taught her how to get out of this. She tried to focus through the distraction of Gideon's hands on her. He told her to flap her wings. She caught his mouth with hers and kissed him hard. She used his own game of distraction against him and started flapping her wings.

They were off the ground quickly. She used the momentum to flip him over on the ground before flying up in the air. He laughed again.

"I love your style." He grinned.

"I thought you might." She said as she landed back on the ground.

"It's an interesting tactic. Either you get the upper hand and kill someone or I see you kissing someone and I kill them." He shrugged as she laughed out loud.

"I wouldn't be kissing anyone else!" she

swatted him on the arm.

"Better not." He grabbed her into his arms.

She braced for a moment, expecting it to be a tactic, but relaxed when he kissed her again. She closed her eyes and enjoyed being fully in the moment with him. He still made her nervous, mate or not. She ran her hand over his chest and felt the muscles underneath his shirt. It clung to him tightly, his skin lightly coated in sweat from fighting.

He picked her up and she wrapped her legs around his waist. They kissed as he walked toward the fountain and sat her down on the edge of it. He kissed her deeply as her butt slipped back and dipped into the water. She inhaled quickly, not expecting the cold sensation.

"You got me wet." She said in between breaths.

"That's what I've been trying to do." He laughed before pulling her tank top strap down and kissing her collarbone.

"What if someone sees us?" She

whispered.

"Cast something around us." He replied, not seeming to be concerned either way.

She was about to cast some sort of invisibility around them when Gideon's phone started chirping. It sounded like someone was sending a lot of text messages all at once. He groaned into Brynn's neck, still pushed up against her. He pulled his phone out and looked at the screen.

"Raef." He said.

"See what he wants." Brynn replied still out of breath.

Gideon looked down at his phone and began scrolling through the messages.

"Is everything ok?" Brynn asked, bracing herself for more drama, but Gideon just laughed.

"He's fine. I guess this is what happens when you have a crush on a girl and get a phone all at the same time."

"Aww. That's sweet. Take it easy on him." Brynn laughed.

"I guess Ecco agreed to train with him. He didn't come out and say it, but it sounds like he got his ass handed to him."

He typed something back quickly and shoved the phone in his pocket. He wanted to get back to where they left off, but Brynn wiggled out from under him. He turned around and raised an eyebrow at her.

"We need to train, silly man." She laughed as she tried to wring some of the water out of her pants.

"Yeah, yeah. We can get back to training, but you have to promise me something."

"Go on." She said with a tone of intrigue.

"We go out on that date tomorrow night. Just say yes and I'll take care of the rest."

"Absolutely." She replied.

"Let's hurry it up then, I'm gonna kick your butt so we can go to bed."

She laughed as she lunged at him. She was a little quicker than before. With each attempt, she got sharper and faster.

"There she is." He said once she stopped struggling. "Welcome back."

"Good to be back." She said as she finally got the upper hand on him.

They continued training for another hour or so before Brynn was finally satisfied with her performance. Gideon was relieved to go inside and rest. Some days he was truly impressed with the amount of energy she had.

"If you were a shifter, I swear you would be a hummingbird or something." He said as they made their walk back to the house.

"What?" she laughed. "Why a hummingbird?"

"I don't know. It's just always buzzing around, flapping those wings as fast as it can. It must take a lot of stamina. Seems like you."

He shrugged his shoulders.

"I'll take it. I think they represent resilience or something anyway."

They walked quietly though the house, surprised that they didn't see anyone else. They must all be resting up for training tomorrow. Brynn hoped they would have a good turnout. She wanted to stop by her parent's room on the way to hers, but she didn't. They both needed their rest. Despite her best attempts, her mom looked exhausted.

"You want to take a shower?" Gideon asked Brynn when they made it to their room.

"Only if you take one with me." She winked at him.

"Ohhhh baby. Say no more." He said before quickly disappearing into the bathroom.

She chuckled as she locked their bedroom door and turned their bed down. She had a strategic plan: from the shower straight to the bed. Gideon's plan probably varied slightly, but not as much as he might think.

"You shower is ready, my queen." He called to her from the bathroom.

Gideon appeared in the bathroom doorway. He had taken off everything but his boxers, which hung low. Very low. He watched Brynn's eyes travel down to his waistband. She blushed and looked up quickly to find him watching her. Busted.

She smiled awkwardly and scurried into the bathroom. He closed the door behind her and locked it.

"No one's getting a show tonight except for me." He said low as she started to undress. "How did I get so lucky?"

She giggled as she removed the last of her clothing. He followed suit.

"You really do deserve to be Queen. You know that right?" he whispered into her ear.

He had her boxed into the corner of the shower, one hand on either side of her. The hot water pouring down his shoulders onto her.

"I still think you're crazy. I'm not fit to

rule all mystica. I don't even know how to handle all of the fairies."

"That's why you have me. I won't let you fail."

"How can you be so sure?"

"Because I know how much faith I have in you. And I know how amazing you are."

She didn't argue any more. There was no changing his mind. She just enjoyed the rest of the shower with Gideon. When they sunk into bed afterward, she was relieved. She was ready for easier days.

He held her close, sticking his nose into the nape of her neck. He inhaled her scent deeply. If only she knew what it did to him. Now that she was his, it was even more intense.

TWENTY THREE

"Is dad awake?" Brynn asked at her parents' bedroom door as soon as it was late enough to be appropriate.

"Yes, sweetheart. Come on in." Shyan said as she ushered Brynn inside the room.

She noticed the bite marks on her mom's neck. It must have helped because Vincent was sitting up in bed. He looked extra pale.

"Hey, dad." Brynn spoke softly.

"Sorry I missed your meeting. I heard how much everyone loved you." He smiled, clearly proud of his daughter.

"It was so uncomfortable." She rolled her eyes as she sat down on the edge of the bed.

"Don't resist it. They are your people now. You have to learn how to embrace it and understand them. There is good and bad to each race. Fairies included but we both knew that already."

"When do you think you will be well?"

"Nice way to change the topic." Vincent laughed. "Later today or tomorrow. Bruce helped me a lot. Are *you* holding up ok? I know that was a traumatic thing to experience."

"I'm ok. I'd rather move past it than talk about it."

"I get it, kiddo. I'm here if you ever do want to discuss it."

"I know you are. I gotta go get ready to train. Let me know if you need anything."

"Let everyone know that I will see them tomorrow."

"Will do." She said as she got up and left the room.

She walked to the kitchen to grab a bite to eat before any visitors arrived. Gideon was already making himself a plate when she walked in.

"How's your pops?" He asked with a mouthful of bacon.

"Better today. He said he'll be good to go tomorrow,"

"Awesome. I figured Catman would get him feeling better."

They scarfed their breakfast quickly and waited for people to arrive. There wasn't much of a plan going in to today. They were planning on playing it by ear and hoping for the best. Luckily for them, everything began to fall into place once people started arriving.

The turnout was good. There were at least twenty people from each race. Brynn was relieved to see so many people interested in being a part of this. At the same time, it meant a lot of mystica crammed in one place that might not like each other so much. Just because everyone knew it was for the greater good didn't mean that the rivalries just went away. Vampires and wolves still didn't like each other much. Elementals didn't trust anyone. The fairies were joining in but still had an air of pretentiousness about them.

Nevertheless, everyone managed to put their feelings aside and train. From the first to arrive to the last to depart, training lasted about five hours. Most left with the promise of returning the next day. Hopefully more people would come as well.

"Meet me in the shower?" Gideon whispered in Brynn's ear once they called it a day.

She smiled and nodded her head, still trying to catch her breath. Today had been a challenge. Thank God she trained with Gideon last night. She would have been embarrassed by her performance otherwise.

"I'll make sure everyone sees themselves out." Raef said to Brynn. "I know my brother has something planned."

"Thank you. I promised we would make time for this."

"Have fun. Don't do anything I wouldn't do." He laughed as she walked into the house.

As promised, she made a beeline to the shower. Gideon already had the water hot and flowing for them. To her surprise, he didn't try too much funny business. In fact, he seemed like he was in a hurry.

"What are we doing tonight?" she asked as she towel dried her hair.

"It's a surprise. But we are starting out at C's Place for dinner."

"The human restaurant downtown?"

"Yep. I can't tell you anything after that though. You will have to wait and find out. You will want to wear sandals though. And maybe a dress or something. That's all I'm gonna say."

She took note of his suggestions and started getting ready. She was very curious what he had in store for them. The amount of effort he was putting into this date was sweet. He knew how to make a girl feel desired. That's for sure.

She threw on a little makeup, dried her hair, and picked out a dress and sandals. Gideon emerged from the closet wearing khaki cargo shorts, boat shoes, and a button up shirt that accentuated his muscles. He gave her a catcall and she did a quick little spin for him.

"Nice dress."

"Thanks. My boyfriend recommended I wear a dress this evening." She laughed before spritzing on a little perfume. "I'm ready when you are, stud."

He ushered her out of the room. Once they made it to the truck, he rushed ahead and opened the door for her. He blocked the view as she climbed up in the truck, making sure no one got a chance to sneak a peek up her dress.

"Have you eaten at this place before?" she asked on the drive.

"No, but I've heard good things. It's supposed to be like Italian meets southern comfort food."

"Sounds interesting."

When they got there, she was surprised to see that it was exactly how he'd described. The menu had quite a blend of comfort food with Italian twists. They decided to order two entrees to share: one chicken Parmesan mac n cheese and deep friend ravioli with creamy Parmesan sauce. They both ordered sweet tea, which they were happy to see had unlimited free refills.

She glanced around, admiring the decor as they waited for their food. It was rustic inside. Ornate stained glass lamp shades hung over each table. There were lots of wooden pieces and details. When the waiter brought the food to the table, the smell made Brynn's mouth water. He topped off their drinks before disappearing back into the restaurant.

They each took a bite of food and instantly made a noise. They laughed at each other.

"I think it's safe to say we like the food." Brynn joked once she swallowed the bite of food she was working on.

They worked their way through the plates, going back and forth between the two dishes. She didn't know which she liked the best. Once they were done, they ordered dessert. Cookie butter cheesecake. It was decadent. She thought about how nice it was to have a boyfriend that liked to eat.

"What's next? A nap?" She joked on the way to the truck.

"It's still a surprise. It will be a little bit of a drive, so there will be time for the food to settle. Don't worry."

She hopped into the truck and started searching for music to listen to.

After they had been in the truck for a while, Gideon turned the music down.

"I have a weird request."

"Ok." She replied hesitantly.

"Can you close your eyes for a little

while?”

"I can do that. Wake me up if I fall asleep, though. I'm still full from dinner."

"Deal." He agreed as she closed her eyes and he pulled off of the main road.

Once they were close to their destination, he rolled the windows down.

"I'll tell ya what. If you can sniff out where we are, you can open your eyes before we get there."

She grinned as she sat up in her seat. She loved a challenge. It was extra breezy. She stuck her nose close to the window and inhaled. The air smelled fresh and almost... salty.

"We're at the beach!" She exclaimed as she opened her eyes.

"I figured this would be a good surprise."

"The best." She bounced up and down in her seat.

She never got to come to the beach. It

was her favorite place to just sit and reflect. For her, there was no better place. Gideon found a spot between the sand dunes and puled the truck over. He hopped out and hurried over to Brynn's side of the truck. He stuck out his hand to help her out of the truck.

"Watch your step. This sand makes a big drop off."

She climbed down and shoved her bare feet in the sand. He closed the truck door behind her and grabbed her hand in his.

"You feel like going for a walk?" he asked as he threw his shoes into the bed of the truck.

"Yes. Let's get close to the water."

He led her down to the shore where the wet sand was easier to walk on. There wasn't much of a moon in the sky, but the stars seemed to shine extra bright. The water crashed back and forth on the shore, rolling in far enough to get her feet wet about every third time. The wind whipped back and forth in periodic gusts.

It was loud and quiet at the same time. The wind and the waves produced volume, but there was nothing else. Just the serene symphony of mother nature. Brynn tilted her head back and enjoyed the song.

They eventually stopped walking and stood with their feet in the water. Gideon stared out into the darkness, far beyond what anyone could see this late at night. Brynn looked up at him. Her tattoo began to softly vibrate. He was nervous about something.

He looked down at her and smiled before turning to face her.

"I love everything about you, Brynn. Your thoughtfulness, your zest for life. You want to take care of everyone and everything. Always willing to play whatever role is needed. You really are amazing and I'm so lucky the stars paired us together.

You being spellbound was one of the scariest things I have ever experienced. I don't ever want to be without you. I have wanted you from the moment I saw you. That day I went home and everything changed. My world began to revolve around you then and you didn't even know it. Even if you weren't my mate, I would still feel this way. The mate bond just makes it stronger."

Gideon dropped down to one knee. Brynn stopped breathing, unable to do anything but stare at him.

"I love you Brynn. I want the entire world to know that you're mine and I want to make it official in every way possible. Will you marry me?"

The waves crashed against him and he pulled a tiny blue velvet box out of his pocket. When he opened it, a single square-shaped moonstone solitaire shined in the starlight. The gem was lined with a row of tiny triangular clear quartz and a row of triangular rose quartz that fit within each other. It was unlike any ring she had ever seen before.

"Yes." She somehow managed to get out before extending her hand for him. "I love you, Gideon. With all my heart." She bent her head down and kissed him.

Thunder boomed suddenly and lightning cracked through the sky, going from star to star until it looked like a giant connect the dots puzzle. Gideon stood quickly, pulling Brynn close to him. In an instant, they were enveloped in bright white light. They had to squint their eyes quickly.

"One last gift." A tiny voice said in Brynn's ear.

A familiar searing pain shot across her collarbone opposite of her constellation tattoo. Once the light subsided, they both took a deep breath. They immediately looked at each other.

"We both have one, right?" She asked as she stared at his collarbone.

"It looks like it." He rubbed his finger over hers. "Yours is a circle. It's kinda oblong, like an oval really."

Of course they were the same.

"Yours is too. Did you hear anything in the light?"

"Nope, but I'm guessing you did. What did you hear?"

"One last gift."

Gideon chuckled. Sometimes he wondered if this was all just a game to the stars. He reached into his pocket and pulled the jewelry box back out. In all the commotion, he shoved it back in there to keep it safe.

"So do you wanna wear this thing or not?" he joked as he opened the box.

Brynn stuck her hand out and he slid it onto her finger. It was a perfect fit. It sparkled beautifully in the starlight. They found a soft spot to sit a short distance from the shore that was barely far enough to stay dry. They snuggled close to each other to stay warm in the evening gulf breeze. A comfortable silence hung in the air and Brynn rested her head on Gideon's broad shoulder.

"Are you sure I'm not in over my head?" She asked quietly.

He turned to look at her before lightly grabbing her chin with his fingers.

"Baby... you are so much more than you realize. You are smart, loyal, and just an overall bad ass. I will always be honest with you. If I thought there was a chance that this might be too much, I wouldn't hesitate to say something. I know that you have this in the bag."

She smiled and he kissed the tip of her nose.

TWENTY FOUR

"Hey Fi. I know things are messed up, but I miss you. It's never too late and I won't give up on you." She hit send knowing the message would go unanswered. It always went through though, so she knew that Fiona was getting them.

Brynn was mad at her sister. She meant what she said, though. It wasn't too late. Yes, she broke the cardinal rule. Max should have been off limits. Deep down though, she felt responsible for everything. Maybe this was her karma.

She needed to stop getting distracted.

It was hard to believe that two weeks had passed since everyone started training together. They had gone by so quickly. So many more people had shown up after the first couple of days. They had a full house a few days each week now. Once Vincent was feeling better, he was fully emerged in leading the training efforts. He was locked in with Daveson when Bruce strode onto the field.

"How's my favorite warlock today?" Vincent asked when he looked up. "Give me five?" he asked Daveson.

"I've come to inform you of my temporary departure. After consulting with a few other warlocks..." He cleared his throat before continuing. "I have decided to take a trip out west to attempt to gain answers. There is chatter about an old kind of magic that can be used against demons. The reservation is going to be the best place to find the information we need."

"Have your cohorts ever dealt with anything like this before?" Vincent asked, surprised to hear of the departure.

"Unfortunately not. They had all heard

stories, but from people who are no longer with us to speak about it. I believe without the tribe's help; we will be going in blind no matter what we do."

"How long do you think it might take?"

"I'm not entirely sure. It will likely take a while to earn the tribe's trust. I won't gain information without that."

"Let us know if we can help you at all, Catman." Gideon patted him on the shoulder as he walked up to the conversation with Brynn in tow.

"Just keep an eye on Maddie while I'm gone. Keep her safe. I worry about her. She hasn't had an easy life."

"You have my word." He agreed.

Brynn's phone rang and she stepped away from the conversation. It was Adrienne, the Luna. Brynn let it go to voicemail. She already knew what the call would be about. To her silent behest, Adrienne had been hard at work planning some sort of ceremony. She wanted to politely decline, but she knew that wasn't an option. Either way, tonight was the night.

She knew it was silly but deep down, she wished Fiona would be there. Not the new, evil Fiona. The sister she got to have a wonderful, brief moment of time with. It seemed like such a cruel thing for it to have been so short lived. Unfair at the very least.

When she turned back around, Bruce was gone. She looked across the training field and chuckled when she saw Raef and Ecco training together. Gideon glanced at her, wondering what she was laughing at.

"Well, it looks like his persistence has paid off." She laughed, raising her hand above her eyes to shield herself from the sun.

Gideon turned to look at his brother. He was amused. Raef was a good fighter, but Ecco appeared to be much faster than him. Lighter on her feet too. She was running circles around Raef and all he could do was smile. Bless his heart.

"I spoke to her when she got here." Brynn cleared her throat. "Alec has been tracking Fiona. He thinks he might have a lead on who was helping Max. He is supposed to check back in by the end of the week.”

“Fantastic. Sounds like they got right to work. Speaking of work, why don’t we knock off a few minutes early? It’s a half day anyway.”

“Ugh. Don’t remind me.” She put her palm on her forehead. “I’m already ready for it to be over.”

“Relax a little. You might actually have a good time.”

She rolled her eyes and smiled. He was probably right. She wasn’t ready to admit that yet, though. She drug her feet.

“Come on. I picked out a dress for you. If we head back now, you can give me a fashion show.” He winked at her.

He was so thoughtful, but he was still such a guy. Always hitting on her and tossing around innuendos. She would typically roll her eyes at him or smack him. The truth was, she liked it. It was flattering. Gideon grabbed her hand and pulled her toward the house with him.

When they got to their room, there was a dress laid out on the bed. When did he even have time to do this? Brynn picked up the dress and twirled it around. It was silky and white with a large, fluffy skirt.

"It will look great with your wings."

"You think I should have them out? They get in the way."

"Hell yeah I do! Be proud of those things, girl. They make you different. You're special. Don't let anyone forget it."

She had to admit, Gideon was a good hype man. She hopped in the shower and started getting ready. Gideon joined her and did a good job distracting her. He knew how nervous she was to be on display like this. He could feel it himself. She was going to shine, though.

He dressed to the nines as well, opting for a dark blue suit. He pulled his hair back, revealing his freshly shaved sides.

"When did you shave your hair off?" Brynn asked, looking at him in the mirror.

"This morning before you woke up. Whatcha think?"

"It's pretty hot." She said with a mischievous grin.

She could have sworn she saw him blush a little. She finished her makeup before running a waver through her hair.

"How do I look?" she asked as she stood up and spun around.

"Perfect." He said with a smile.

She closed her eyes for a moment and cast a quick courage spell.

"Don't judge me." She said swiftly.

"No judgment. Do whatever you need to do." He said before taking her hand.

They slowly walked through the house. No one else appeared to be inside the house. As they got close to the French doors leading to the garden, Brynn could see lights outside. A cool late summer breeze hit her in the face once Gideon opened the doors. She looked around before walking outside.

Where people had been training earlier in the day was now occupied by a large, expensive looking white tent. The walkway was lined with lights. Soft music was playing and you could hear the chatter of people. Brynn's heart started to race as they got close.

Everyone stopped talking when Brynn walked into the tent. She scanned the room, surprised to see everyone dressed in their best. One of the wolves howled and everyone began to cheer. Brynn tried to see who it was, but everyone erupted too quickly.

Tables adorned with white tablecloths and a large mason jar of flowers lined the room. Toward the back were buffet tables full of food. At the pinnacle of the room, was a smaller table with two chairs that had a taller back than the rest. As Brynn looked above, she noticed a lavish chandelier hanging in the center.

Everyone seemed to be having a good time together. After the buffet had been ravaged and the champagne had been flowing for a while, Gideon stood up to make a toast. He gently clinked his knife against the side of his champagne glass. The room became silent and all eyes were on him.

"Tonight, we come together to celebrate Brynn. A woman who has stood up to opposition and looked danger in the eye. She has defended all of us and fought to free our people. In spite of this, she remains humble and hopeful.

The stars have shown her favor. May she always guide us and lead us to victory."

Gideon placed a golden crown upon Brynn's head before kissing her hand and bowing. Everyone followed suit and when every knee was on the ground, the room erupted in a roar. People clapped, some cheered, and the music got loud. It was like an instant party broke out. Suddenly where an empty buffet sat before was a table full of desserts. The champagne had been replaced with a small bar and colorful cocktails.

Once the dancing started, Brynn had a tough time not losing herself in the party. She and Gideon danced close. He kissed her neck and she tilted her head back and giggled. She had to grab her crown quickly to keep it from falling off.

Her constellation tattoo started to hum and she and Gideon looked at each other. Things were a little hazy. She shouldn't have had that drink. Who made it so strong? She squinted her eyes to focus.

"Is she okay?" Jeremy asked as he walked by. "She doesn't look so good."

Ugh. She couldn't stand this guy. He gave her the creeps.

"Danger!" The celestial voice in her head yelled.

Oh no.

"Gideon..." she said in a panicked tone before the music stopped.

Everyone stopped what they were doing when a different song suddenly came on. What song was this? It was new but she had heard it before. Brynn listened to the lyrics for a moment and she realized what it was. Devil in a Dress by Teddy Swims. The bass was up so loud she could feel the beat of the song in the floor.

A puff of black smoke appeared in the

middle of the room almost on cue with the chorus of the song and everyone jumped back. Not Brynn. She steadied her feet. She knew who she was about to see and she refused to back down.

"Fiona." Brynn said as emotionless as she could.

"Happy to see me?" she asked before tilting her head to the side and laughing.

Her black wings were just as big as Brynn's. She was even wearing a little black dress with patent leather stilettos. She looked like Brynn's exact opposite right now. Fiona extended her arm and cast a barrier around the two of them. Gideon charged, trying to get to Brynn but he bounced right off.

"Fiona! No!" Vincent bellowed before trying to get to his daughters.

His attempt was as useless as Gideon's. No one was prepared for Fionas strength. All of Brynn's tattoos burned and the frequency in her ears was so high, she felt like she might explode.

She had to do something. She tried to

grab the blade she had stashed away in a band around her upper thigh. Fiona saw her motion and snapped her fingers.

"Tisk, tisk." She said before the blade flew into her hand.

She threw the blade through the barrier. It missed Gideon's neck by about an inch.

"You bitch." Brynn spat.

"Next time be more careful what you wish for, sis." Fiona whispered in her sister's ear before wrapping her hand around Brynn's forearm.

"Let me go, Fiona! Stop!"

She tried to yank her arm out of Fiona's grasp, but she couldn't. She had gotten so strong. Brynn could smell a hint of sulfur on her breath. Cold, black eyes stared back at her. This wasn't her sister anymore. She understood that now. Max had turned her into something evil.

"I'm only getting started." She winked.

The music stopped and Fiona sent a shockwave out around her. It knocked everyone down. Gideon and a few other Alphas scrambled to get to their feet. Brynn saw Daveson and Finn shift and start to charge toward her.

"Thanks for coming!" Fiona shouted with a giggle before snapping her fingers.

Three hundred ravens appeared where she and Brynn had been standing. The birds screeched before trying to fly out of the door. Pandemonium broke out. People were getting scratched by the birds as they scrambled to get away.

Daveson and Finn were still in wolf form. They were chasing the birds away from the crowd. Once the feathers settled, the center of the floor was empty.

"BRYNN!" Gideon roared.

But it was too late. She was gone...

PROPHECY OF A FAE

BOOKS ONE AND TWO
NOW
AVAILABLE

ROGUE FAE

BOOK THREE
COMING
SOON

READ AHEAD FOR A SNEAK PEEK

ROGUE FAE
PROLOGUE

"Where am I?" Brynn whispered to herself.

Wherever she was at was pitch black. It was steamy, almost like a sauna. She tried to focus on what was going on around her. She couldn't hear anything, but there was a smell that was getting stronger.

Sulfur. Damn.

This wasn't good. She knew why that hole and her sister smelled like sulfur. Demons.

Where had Fiona taken her? And more importantly, how was she going to get out of here? She concentrated hard on what she had been calling the "angel radio" in her head.

"Can anyone hear me? SOS." She thought hard.

"You can't stay there. Get moving."

Thank God there was an answer. Was that Aeriethrael?

"Yes. It is me. You are going to have to find your inner light if you hope to find your way out. But be warned. Once you activate your light, you will be able to see each other. Beware."

"What does that mean?"

Aeriethrael didn't say anything else. Brynn sat there for another moment contemplating. She was going to have to figure out the light thing. She didn't like that warning, though. What was she going to see?

She didn't know how to do this. She kept thinking about light but nothing was happening.

"I'll take some tips if you want to give me any." She thought.

There was still no answer.

She started feeling a little panic. Could Gideon feel her distress wherever she was? She subconsciously rubbed the newest tattoo on her collarbone. She had been affectionately referring to it as her marriage tattoo due to the shape and timing of it.

There it was... her light. It started off dim but was slowly growing. She focused hard on the light and tried to control it. If it got too bright too fast, she still wouldn't be able to see. Not to mention others would be able to see her more easily since that was going to be a thing apparently.

She looked down at the floor beneath her.

* 9 7 9 8 9 8 9 8 9 0 0 3 3 *